Humanity's Hinge

J. A. Dawson

Disclaimer

This is a work of fiction. Unless otherwise indicated, all the names, characters, businesses, places, events and incidents in this book are either the product of the author's imagination or used in a fictitious manner. Any resemblance to actual persons, living or dead, or actual events is purely coincidental.

Copyright © J. A. Dawson, 2024

For Dianne

Table of Chapters

-1- 6
-2- 12
-3- 21
-4- 27
-5- 36
-6- 43
-7- 51
-8- 61
-10- 73
-11- 78
-12- 86
-13- 92
-14- 102
-15- 108
-16- 120
-17- 126
-18- 133
-19- 140
-20- 151
-21- 159
-22- 172
-23- 181
-24- 191

-25-	*203*
-26-	*212*
-27-	*218*
-28-	*226*
-29-	*240*

Northern France, September 6th, 1917

02:30 hrs

Slowly, steadily, the world came back to him. There was a dryness in his mouth and throat that made him retch a little as he breathed in a lungful of chill air. He could feel a moistness from what he assumed was grass on and around his fingers and could vaguely detect a slow permeation of dampness through the thick serge material, to his shins. He realised he was kneeling, hands forward, on all fours. He remained that way for a little while, unmoving other than the shallow inhalation-exhalation of his breathing. He couldn't have done any more, even if he'd wanted to. It wasn't for lack of strength, he was sure, but more due to an intense feeling, akin to being drunk. His head swam with a dizzying vertigo, so that all he could do was concentrate on staying where he was, hoping it would pass quickly. As the waves of nausea began to subside, he had the vague notion that he was cold; perhaps that too would pass, though something in his mind seemed to promise otherwise.

After what seemed to be several minutes, he slowly eased himself rearwards, still kneeling, but resting more upright, with his buttocks pressing back on his heels. The slow, wet saturation from the ground was starting to make his knees feel uncomfortable, but it was still far too early for anything as adventurously bold as standing. Instead, he chanced some head movement, slowly acclimatising to his surroundings. His mind began linking things together, remembering that it would be dark; although he could not recall it ever being *this* dark. He could barely see more than three metres, just about making out the long grass in all directions; the dense, ominous shapes of hedgerows that projected away, out of view. As he adjusted his vision to the gloom, he was aware of an intense sensation at the back of his neck; an unremitting desire, no, an essential need, to scratch – and scratch hard. Moving his arm gingerly up, his fingers pulled the coarse collar aside, seeking out the offending itch. Yes, it was coming back to him: the bloody material. Whomever had invented it must have had an agenda, though why that should be to generate insatiable discomfort, he could not begin to speculate.

As well as the gentle sound of the breeze, he could just make out a low hubbub of noise coming from his left. From that direction, in the distance, a slightly luminous glow seemed to grow out of the horizon - what could only be, in this darkness, habitation. Feeling, rather than seeing, he took stock of himself. Cutting diagonally across his chest, the strap of a bag, a sharp buckle, digging into his sternum. Clothed all over, it seemed, in the same itchy, coarse material as his collar and, as his fingers explored his sleeves, cuffs and shoulders, he felt two raised pips on his epaulettes that brought his memories into view. Two pips, he recalled, indicated the rank of lieutenant.

OK, he thought, *time to stand up.*

Pulling himself up to a squat, as if ready for the starter's gun, he tested the strength of his thighs. Satisfied he was prepared, he pushed himself up to his full height. It was a mistake. He couldn't remember what he'd had for his last meal, nor could he see it in the murk; but up it came, nevertheless. The noise of his heaving, though not overly loud, was enough to disturb the birds roosting in the nearby bushes; he cursed them, and himself, for their racket as they took flight with a clattering of wings. He was hardly exhibiting any intended stealth so far. Wiping his mouth on his sleeve, he actually felt much better, more stable on his feet. Searching his bag, he located the expected cap and, putting it on, began to walk slowly towards the light glow.

The air was definitely different. Every breath seemed to cut deep into the lungs, though not unpleasantly. It was a cold inhalation, not unlike the feel of breathing in clouds of dry ice vapour. Complementing this alien experience, the night sky was inky black, a darkness so full that even shadows were largely absent. This took some getting used to, often tripping on unseen stones and potholes along, what felt like, a road he had come to. As he walked, his mind knitted these observations together. He was outside, that was a start; the air was significantly chillier; there was virtually no light pollution – all of this signified that the experiment had worked. He smiled to himself, self-indulgently.

I can't believe it. It bloody worked.

The light glow up ahead was steadily becoming brighter. This meant contact; this meant speaking, interacting. If he couldn't land this, it would have all been for nothing. Recalling what was ahead, he began to search his pockets. His fingers closed around a firm piece of card, which he held tightly, feeling its security. As the light increased in brightness, he began to make out more distinct shapes: some kind of tower; the square profiles of buildings and, closer still, two standing figures, just starting to move, as he approached. He felt the nausea building again and gulped down mouthfuls of air in an effort to staunch the gyrations in his stomach.

I really need to hold it together now.

The men in front of him took shape. Both wore similar attire to him, the only two differences were that both wore steel helmets, as opposed to his cap, and -- more ominously -- both of them were armed. As he drew closer, the nearest one shoulder-slung his rifle and snapped his feet together, the boots making a loud crack in the night silence.

'Good evening, sir.' He called, far too loudly for the distance between them. His right arm shot upwards, smartly, in a crisp salute.

The lieutenant mirrored the action, producing what he hoped was a convincing, more casual, officer-style effort. Looking over the guard's shoulder, he could see the other soldier, rifle carried loosely, but, nevertheless, looking on cautiously. A pregnant pause followed, and the guard looked expectantly into the lieutenant's eyes. He said nothing, which magnified the awkwardness of the moment, clearly signifying that *something* should be happening, but wasn't. Despite the cool breeze, the officer began to feel a prickle of sweat forming in-between his shoulder blades. After what seemed an age, the guard spoke again.

'May I see your I.D. please sir?'

Of course, what a bloody idiot. He'd been holding it in readiness for the last half kilometre.

'Yes, of course.' Was what he'd meant to say - was the only suitable answer, really. It did not come out that way. Instead, a croaked, scratchy version of the words were the result; words from someone who has not used their voice, seemingly, for years. He scolded himself for not limbering up his vocal chords ahead of the encounter. He saw a glaze of doubt momentarily pass over the guard's eyes, quickly replaced by concentration as he scrutinised the offered card, held up for inspection. Satisfied, the guard again fired up another whip-crack salute and, trying to allow the lieutenant some sympathy for his hoarse reply, offered some geniality.

'Heavy night was it, sir?' A wry grin and a knowing wink. Again, the pregnant pause as the lieutenant tried to knit meanings together. Then it dawned on him. He scrabbled around internally for an answer. After way too long, he replied, falteringly.

'Err, yes, you could say that. One too many at Le Jardin...'.

As soon as he'd spoken, he knew it was all wrong. He damned himself again. *Too much information, you idiot; no-way would an officer offer such conversation to a private he didn't know.* He looked into the guard's eyes and, this time, saw consternation descend like a cloud.

'How is it you're coming from this way then sir?'

Shit.

In an instant, he realised the problem. Le Jardin d'Eden was one of two brothels in Étaples town that he had researched - what felt like a thousand years ago. Though he did not know what the local time was, he'd cleverly -- or so he'd thought -- dropped on the idea that the brothel would be the kind of establishment for which a 'closing time' would not have applied. *Rather ingenious in a pinch*. The problem, therefore, was an obvious one: this checkpoint was clearly on the wrong side of camp to be coming from the town. His brain worked furiously; he contemplated whether to justify himself by explaining how he needed to walk off a drunken state; was this feasible? He had no idea how long the perimeter of the camp was, though he knew the area to be huge in size. He decided to take a more realistic approach.

'When I want questions from you, I shall bloody well ask for them, private.' He said, caustically.

As if turning a switch, the guard's hesitancy evaporated, replaced by the robotic obedience of the professional soldier.

'Yes sir, sorry sir.'

The private stepped aside, bringing himself to attention, planting his right heel down with a hard stamp, the left arm snapping into his side. The lieutenant walked on past, glowering at the second guard, who also adopted the required stance in readiness. Through the raised barrier he walked, on into the silent camp.

London, April 10th, 2142

10:18 hrs

Barrett pulled the hessian cover over the body. He was accustomed to seeing cadavers, but rarely someone he actually knew. The deceased had been a fellow police investigator who worked in the same department; a guy called Daniels. He'd always seemed competent enough, had been instrumental in solving several cases Barrett was aware of. Initial evaluation of the scene, however, suggested that Daniels had simply become careless. In pursuing a suspect, he had allowed the 'perp' to descend several floors down from street level, past the areas considered safe for ordinary citizens, into the sub-layers of the city where the weapon detection grid was patchy. Clearly, there had been a hidden gun, left lying in wait, ready to reach for, as the cop closed in. Examining the dead man's wounds, it was clear to Barrett that the murder weapon had been an old-fashioned pistol of some kind. The bullets had left quite small, neat entry holes, but their route out again had left a hell of a mess. Of course, there had been no witnesses, not down here. It wasn't that the sub-levels were considered a no man's land, but visitors to these layers did so through necessity, rather than desire. They housed a huge network infrastructure, mainly comprising the complex geothermal grids that heated the population's homes above; such systems needed to be maintained, checked, repaired and so forth, and thus the main frequenters tended to be engineers, but not today.

Standing over the body, Barrett looked up and down the alleyway where the murder had taken place. Steam jetted out of leaky pipework joints, where the intense heat had ruptured seals. Looking back down, Barrett could see the dead man was lain at an acute angle, as if he had been trying to touch his toes from a prone position. There was no way of determining the direction of firing from this orientation; ballistic weapons, Barrett knew, were powerful, and could throw a person off their feet, sometimes propelling them some distance, sometimes even swiveling them around by the sheer kinetic impact, depending on the calibre and muzzle velocity of the weapon used. All of this was unknown, at this stage. Just beyond Daniels' body, Barrett could make out some blood spattering, a random pattern decorating the pathway. Kneeling down, he followed the direction of the spray outwards, imagining the effect of the round leaving the body, taking some of Daniels' blood with it, gauging where the suspected trajectory pointed. Some ten metres or so beyond the blood, Barrett could see a Mallocrete wall. Carefully navigating around the carnage, ignoring the busy comings and goings of the cordon officers and the forensic team, unpacking their equipment, Barrett walked up to the wall. Though difficult to see in the darkened sub-level lighting, there in front of him, around half a metre up from the ground, was a small indentation showing where one of the rounds had punctured into the wall material. Reaching for his back pocket, he withdrew his console, a small handheld device that performed a wide variety of functions. As a police console, his did a whole lot more than the common, garden variety version. He pressed a sequence of buttons, selecting the scan function, and hovered the device over the pock mark, before pressing the button on the side to engage the analysis. The scanner head inside the smooth, thin case, oscillated three times and then gave a satisfying beep, informing him its task was complete. Isolating and discarding the organic composition of the wall itself, the read-out gave a detailed breakdown of the remnant round's metallurgical data. Alas, Barratt mused, there was no way it could isolate anything else. There was no DNA return. He hadn't really banked on it: the high energy impact would have obliterated any trace.

Too bad. But. What if...?

Rubbing his chin thoughtfully, Barrett looked back down the length of the alleyway. Applying what the police training school used to call visualisation, he pictured, in his mind's eye, the weapon, spitting fire with an explosive roar; he remembered the acrid smell of burning cordite he'd had the pleasure of experiencing at a once attended historical show. Barrett's passion for history, particular the world wars of the twentieth century, had been something of an obsession for many years, a pastime that had threatened his marriage on more than one occasion. And while it was highly likely that the murder weapon used here was not a relic from those eras, it was, nevertheless, a breach-loading, combustion-ballistic device, utilising the ignition of gunpowder in a cartridge casing to propel the bullet forward. That shell casing, he had seen first-hand, was *always* ejected away, making way for the next round to be fed into the firing chamber. Could the perp have been careless too?

Locking the metallurgical composition of the round into the console, he reset the gain on the scanner, extending the range to its full thirty metre maximum. Turning the console back towards the body, he pressed the execute key once more. On the second sweep, the scanner signified a match, automatically sending out a focused laser light, surgically locating a point some several metres further up the alleyway. Following the laser beam, Barrett walked to where it was targeting a semi-sunken storm drain. Crouching down, he craned his head to peer inside. The laser, still persisting in its quest to find its target, reflected brightly off the brass casing like a lighthouse beacon. Barrett smiled. Pulling on a single forensic glove from a sealed packet, he reached in and pulled the cartridge casing out. Holding it delicately, he used the scanner yet again, reset to a broader scope. This time the beep signaled the sweet reward of a DNA trace, deposited unknowingly as the shooter had loaded the bullet into the weapon. Two more presses and the device displayed the DNA's 'owner'. The 'perp's face, name, address, likely accomplices, everything.

'Got you.' Barrett said to himself, with satisfaction.

In swift succession, several more button presses of his console summoned a quick reaction team to locate and 'apprehend with extreme caution'. Granted, it was prejudicial to conclude that the same person who *loaded* the weapon, also *fired* the weapon, but there were ways to confirm this too, once the perp was in custody. He deposited the casing into the same bag the glove had come from and walked back to his vehicle.

Around an hour later, Barrett's console purred serenely, as he was seating himself back behind his desk at the Police Department. The screen displayed the caller: a mugshot of the Chief Investigator, from a much earlier time: his hair still dark, and at least fifteen kilos lighter. Barrett glanced down the length of the room to where the Chief's private office was situated, behind near-permanently closed doors. *Perhaps if he got off his arse now and then and actually walked around to see his staff, he wouldn't look so different from his telephoto*, he thought, uncharitably. He swiped the select banner to accept the call.

'Yes, Chief.'

'I need to see you right away; something has come up.' The Chief's voice sounded more anxious than usual. Barrett pushed himself back on his chair with resignation; why did he just know it was going to be related to the 'apprehend' he had called in, earlier.

'On my way.' He said, tapping the end call motif.

As he eased around his crowded desk, he glanced down at his lunch: a sealed foil bag with the words, 'Roast Chicken Deli Sandwich' on the side. Two things came to mind. The first thought was that he doubted there had ever been a chicken, roasted or otherwise, anywhere near that sandwich. The second was that he doubted he would get to a lunch, of any kind. It was going to be one of those days.

The Chief sat behind his desk studying the screen of a larger version console, holding it in one meaty paw. At a glance it was clear that he was perturbed. His collar was splayed, shirt cuffs rolled up, a sweaty sheen glinted across his forehead – all the usual signs that he was not having a good day. Barrett inwardly brushed off any hope that the Chief was going to congratulate him on his earlier detective work. As he sat down, after waiting for an invitation that hadn't been offered, the Chief continued to examine the console's contents. Making his subordinate wait. It was an age-old routine, Barrett contemplated with mild annoyance. The Chief would speak when he was good and ready. So be it.

Barrett took the opportunity to look around the room. It was in dire need of a clear out. Empty disposable coffee mugs littered the floor, overflowing from the waste bin. An old picture of the Chief shaking hands with some senior official was on the wall, but it was so badly tilted, it was clear that it meant a whole lot less than it had done. The Chief's desk was a total disaster, with piles of data packs, precipitously stacked, one upon the other, the whole lot dangerously close to falling onto the floor. The Chief himself was the human equivalent of the room. His pallor was a shade redder than healthy; his hair lacked any vitality and looked in serious need of some conditioner. Barrett inwardly smiled at this, imagining the Chief being whisked through the 'Big Reveal' curtain to meet the 'Make-Over' live, studio audience. As he fought off a grin, he was brought back to reality, by the Chief peering over the top of his console, fixing him with an accusatory stare.

'Can you give me any clue as to why you have been called to a meeting in Horizon HQ? A meeting that includes Horizon's CEO *and* the Senior Government Supervisor?'

OK, Barrett thought, *so, nothing to do with the apprehend shout.*

Barrett slumped back in the chair, with a suitably confused expression.

'Absolutely no idea, Boss.' The Chief liked it when people called him Boss. Barrett hoped that this was a testing question, that he was about to be told *exactly* why he had been summoned to such a meeting. Evidently, this was not to be.

'Well, I don't know either and, it seems, I am not likely to find out!' He spluttered. 'Bloody liberties; pulling my men off their duties and not even giving me the courtesy of explaining why!'

The Chief's face was adding a blotchiness to its already red and puffy appearance. Despite his misgivings, Barrett felt genuinely sorry for him; it was clear that the man was unaccustomed to being left out of the loop. Barrett tried, in vain, to let the Chief know that his first loyalties lay with him, and the Department.

'At least let me finalise the Daniels report first?' Barrett hated leaving work half done; he wanted the case properly executed and, hopefully, tied up tight, with the killer in custody as soon as possible. The Chief shook his head; if anything, the suggestion had made his agitation worse.

'That'll have to wait. Hand your dossier over to Craig. You have been ordered to head straight to Horizon HQ without delay. Whatever it is they want you for, it has gone way above me.'

Above me? So, he had objected, but hadn't obviously got anywhere.

'What really pisses me off is that it has been classified 'eyes-only, top secret'...' He paused, staring Barrett in the eye. '...and you say you've no idea?' He ranted the question, the implication clear that he thought Barrett *did* know something, but wasn't letting on.

This had really got in his craw, Barrett thought. So much so that the Chief was flagrantly at fault: if it *was* so hush-hush to have been tagged top secret, the Chief was breaking the law by even asking questions about it. Barrett waited quietly for the storm to subside. He had no idea what it was all about, and even if he did, he couldn't discuss it here, in any case. Eventually, the Chief tossed the console onto his desk in resignation.

'Go.' He said, miserably.

Northern France, September 6th, 1917

03.30 hrs

Following the uneven track-like roads, carved up into troughs, through a combination of heavy rainfall and loaded carts, the lieutenant navigated his way into the centre of the camp. With military efficiency, signposts had been handily located, their placards rough-sawn into arrow shapes, pointing the way, the wording just barely visible in the dark. To the right, the Bull Ring; to the left, the beach; straight on, Messes and 'compound'. As he walked, he could see great steepled tents rise up out of the ground on either side; they looked reminiscent of small marquees, all thick white canvas, their tight guy ropes pulling in all directions, holding the tents in place against the gradually strengthening winds. Past one of these, he could hear the throaty snoring of some of its inhabitants. On past wooden huts, white painted picket fences and, what could only be -- from the overpowering odour -- a block of latrines. He eventually came to a large, long-sided building surrounded by closely cropped grass and, what looked like, a small rockery. A rectangular, neatly painted sign identified it as his new home: The Officers' Mess.

Inside, he tiptoed his way through the entrance lobby and found his way into a lounge bar area, distinct from the strong aroma of stale beer, signifying perhaps the previous evening's activities. The seating was unsurprisingly luxuriant: several deep seated, bountifully upholstered, Chesterfield couches, the colour unknown in the dark room. The lieutenant gratefully sank into one, the leather sighing beneath his weight. His eyes closed and he quickly became drowsy, listening to the rhythmic, soporific sound of the swinging pendulum of the grandfather clock, in the corner. He slept.

With a start, the shrill sound of a bugle cut through the treacle of his slumber, making him lurch upright, his heart racing. He had no notion of how long he'd been out, but the grandfather clock, which he could now see in the dawning half-light, showed it to be 5 a.m. The cacophony could only be reveille. His mouth had a sticky dryness and he wondered just how loud he'd probably been snoring. Looking around the room, he momentarily contemplated whether he could stomach sipping some of the left-over beer dregs, but seeing the odd pint pot, complete with extinguished cigarette ends, made him gag.

Opening his satchel, he located a wristwatch, which he manually adjusted to the new time, followed by a few rotations of the winder to keep the ancient mechanism running. Next, he searched through the included paper documents, all carefully creased and worn. Locating the one he needed, he folded it up and tucked it into his left breast pocket. Content that he was as prepared as he could be, he made his way back towards the Mess entrance, arriving just in time to see a slightly shabby looking corporal come in through the door. On seeing the lieutenant, the corporal hastily patted himself down, trying forlornly to eliminate the creases in his steward's tunic.

'Good morning, sir. My word, you're early.' Skirting around the reception desk, the corporal quickly opened a leather-bound ledger, spinning it around for the lieutenant and placing a fountain pen on the page for his use.
'Could you please warn-in sir?' The British military parlance for signing into a Mess momentarily gave the lieutenant an anxious pause as he scanned the book for clues. The earlier entries showed him the way and, picking up the pen, he scrawled his name, rank and remembered service number, followed, in the next column, by his real signature, and finally the date. Offering the drafting document, from his breast pocket, along with his I.D. card, the steward shook his head with a slightly bemused smile.
'Oh, that won't be necessary, sir.' He turned around to the wall cabinet behind the desk and extracted a key with a ridiculously large wooden fob attached to it. Accepting the room key, the lieutenant noticed the steward peering past him. 'May I help carry your effects, sir?' Despite there clearly being none to carry. The lieutenant was at least prepared for *this* question. Affecting a perturbed countenance, he replied.

'When they get here, yes. Bloody porters mislaid them from the channel crossing. They should hopefully arrive later today.'

No chance of that, he thought. The steward nodded his understanding.

'Of course, sir. Sorry to hear that.' The steward's gaze drifted down to the lieutenant's damp, discoloured knees. 'Just a suggestion, sir. There are some spare trousers hanging up in the drying room. I think you'll be in luck for a size, should you wish for me to get yours laundered.'

The lieutenant followed the man's stare; true, it was one thing for a corporal to look unkempt, but it wouldn't do for someone holding the King's commission. He smiled in gratitude.

'Yes, thank you corporal, that would be most helpful.' Glancing at the fob and back at the steward, the corporal read the implied inquiry.

'Down that corridor, sir. Fourth door on the left.'

As the lieutenant located his door, the steward's voice called down the corridor to him, in a sort of shouted whisper, careful not to disturb the other slumbering inhabitants.

'Sir, sir...?' and then, as an afterthought: 'Lieutenant...Barrett?'

Barrett swivelled on one heel and looked back at the steward. 'I forgot to mention, sir. Dinner is served at 20.00 hrs.'

Safely behind his door, Barrett exhaled noisily and surveyed his new domain. The room was sparsely furnished, by comparison to the relative opulence of the lounge bar. A single, unmade, iron-framed bed filled one corner. A small writing desk, an uncomfortable looking wooden chair, and a pedestal wash basin leaning against a wall below a tarnished, foggy mirror, were the remaining fittings. *Well, he was hardly on holiday*, he mused to himself. The bedding sat on the mattress in a cube-shaped 'bed pack': the sheets tightly folded and surrounded by blankets, all wrapped up with a counterpane bedspread in a typically military manner of pointlessness that he had read about. The thought of getting some more, much needed, rest was immediately discounted as he thought about how he would have to unpick this geometric puzzle before he could even get his head down. Besides, time was a commodity he did not have. He had a job to do, and the clock was most definitely ticking.

Leaving his satchel on the disgustingly stained mattress, he went back out into the corridor, in search of the drying room, a reconnoitre he would do well to perform, before many more of his fellow 'officers' awoke. Several furtive minutes later, he had acquired not only some reasonably well-fitting trousers, but also two more shirts, some clean puttees and a few pairs of antique undergarments – *beggars can't be choosers*, he thought, hoping their absence would not be too conspicuous.

Back in his room, Barrett looked at his face in the mirror. He certainly looked as fatigued as he felt. Perhaps he could chance just a couple more hours. He had arrived early after all. On top of all that, no one of importance knew he was even here; there was no expectation at all. Yes, one or two hours would help a lot. He glanced again at the bed pack, pushed it unceremoniously onto the floor and flopped down with the abandon that only comes with extreme exhaustion. He slept, without a single movement, for five hours straight.

London, April 10th, 2142

13:15 hrs

Barrett's car moved along the highway in virtual silence, the only noise came from the contact between the wheels and the road surface. He noted, with satisfaction, that the vehicle's on-board battery health indicator showed forty-seven percent and climbing. The highway to Horizon was fully underpinned with an induction loop which topped up the vehicle's charge, just by travelling along it. Not all roads in London had this infrastructure, so he appreciated it when he had the opportunity to use them. He surveyed the other instrument read-outs: outside temperature was a moderate 37 degrees Celsius; air quality, indicated on a colour scale, was a reassuringly deep shade of green: the best it could get. He knew that the closer one got to the city centre, the more efficient the DACS system tended to be. Direct Air Carbon Capture and Storage had been developed in the early 2000s but had not been invested in until emissions had reached a critical state; a state too far gone to save millions of people, as it turned out.

London was a carbon free zone and had been for at least forty years, but that had only been half the battle. After 2070, when things had reached an all-time, cataclysmic low, a few global super corporations, headed by altruistic, billionaire visionaries, had taken the positive, direct action, by dint of sheer financial hegemony, to force humanity into taking responsibility for its habitat. Together they had provided a multi-trillion-dollar economic jump start to quality research, development and implementation of renewable technologies. The sad truth, however, was that this colossal campaign had come far too late. The combination of human selfishness, apathy and extremes of global economic disparity meant that a vast portion of the world's population either didn't care enough to save their environment, or couldn't afford to do anything about it, even if they had wanted to. The enormous imbalance in wealth around the world meant that all many could do was simply try to survive; after all, when sufficient warmth and food were the priority, few cared whether the means to obtain these staples had detrimental effects on an ever-degrading planet. Even with truly enormous investment, the tipping point was such that only certain areas were deemed savable.

Within the former nation state of the United Kingdom, a term long since considered redundant, London had become one such place, along with Birmingham, Manchester and Edinburgh. Within a set perimeter of the cities, vast projects were undertaken to transform the encircled environments. Emissions of all kinds were strictly controlled, then eliminated altogether. Buildings and infrastructure were torn down and rebuilt using sophisticated, green materials and technology. Huge swathes of land were repurposed as green spaces, with abundant plant life installed, acting as natural carbon sinks. Fossil fuel power generation, which had been in decline for decades, was systematically replaced with renewable technologies of supreme design and yield. DACS systems ran alongside geothermal heat generation, solar and wind farm power-production technologies, vastly enhanced electrical storage batteries, all of it developed to create an oasis of sustainability. But, like all oases, they were surrounded by deserts.

Barrett's wife, Monica, had been brought up in the wastelands outside the London barrier. The detective had been investigating illegal shipments of supplies finding their way out of London and onto black markets in the conurbations dotted around the city's outer limits. The couple had fallen in love after she had tended his wounds, following a stake out that had gone horribly awry. He had brought her back to the city and they had married – the only way he could secure her residency. They'd had twelve very happy years, but it was not to last. Though she had left the wasteland, it had not left her. Years of terrible air quality had wrought her lungs asunder, and at the age of only thirty-two, she developed cancer. The disease progressed rapidly once it had taken root in her lymph. Despite so many technological improvements, medical science had not kept pace. She had died within the year.

Barrett, though devastated, bore no ill will to the generations of society that had created the conditions for his tragic loss. The cold, harsh reality was that she had simply been one of literally thousands, dying daily. The people had not been able to sustain their planet, and so, in return, their planet could no longer sustain them. The Earth shrugged them off, like dead fleas from a dog's back. Despite his intense grief, he resolutely believed that the time for self-pity, as a species, could no longer be afforded. He staunchly trusted that a future could still be created, one that could, conceivably, resurrect humanity's chances, and, hard as it was to reconcile, he counted himself lucky, not only to have had love in his life, but that he was one of the tiny few who might still make the Earth liveable again. Him and people like him, doing their duty; trying their very best for those who were forever pushing the boundaries of what was feasible, in efforts to restore a more responsible future. As he pulled his car off the highway, he looked up at the neon-lit sign of one such forward-thinking corporation: Horizon. Unsure as to the part he was being summoned to play, his mind was, nevertheless, open to the possibilities. He felt a buzz of anticipation.

Sat in an all glass waiting room, his eyes took in the scene. Far from being a minimalist, austere surrounding, the space was loaded with hot house plants: flowers, creepers, trailing honeysuckles and flora types with names he couldn't even guess. This little lot would have produced a great deal of precious oxygen, he thought. But likewise, he looked skyward, past the nature, locating the vents built into the ceiling; these were part of the conditioning system which took away carbon dioxide during the night, when the plants breathed for themselves. He was just contemplating how the high placed flora received hydration, when his name was called by a secretary who had appeared through a set of double doors, holding the obligatory clipboard. He followed her, clip-clopping through two long corridors, eventually entering a large boardroom dominated by an impressively long table. Two people rose up from their chairs at the very far end, broad smiles on their faces, like sales representatives.

'Good afternoon, Detective Investigator Barrett, it is a real pleasure to meet with you. My name is Henrik Anders. I am the CEO here at the London branch of Horizon.'

The man was mid-fifties, neatly dressed and coiffured. Like many very successful people, Barrett had met, there appeared to be no spare weight on his frame. And as Barrett approached him, he imagined a very structured daily routine: early rise, a few lengths in the private pool before a healthy breakfast of mineral water and fruit-protein purees. He remembered having to interview a 'company man' once, as part of an investigation. He'd been 'squeezed in' to the businessman's schedule so that Barrett could ask his questions during a routine stakeholder meeting, carried out -- as all his meetings were -- as part of a power walk around the company complex. 'I always conduct my meetings like this...cuts down on the bullshit.' The exec had spouted, somewhat self-importantly. Oh yes, Barrett pondered, excesses of any kind were to be resisted: they could interfere with accomplishment.

Shaking hands with Barrett, the older man motioned to the woman standing beside him.

'And this is Charlotte Pilgrim, Chief Government Supervisor.'

The woman nodded, but said nothing, merely smiled at Barrett; no offered hand this time. The slightly minor-sounding title belied the woman's status; in another time period, she would have held the role that would have been historically closer to Prime Minister, or President. She was a tall, elegantly dressed woman, with a no-nonsense expression. Barrett estimated her to also be in her mid-fifties, and despite her titled position of seniority, she gave off an aura that suggested she liked her intel direct and unembellished. As the three gravitated to the chairs at the end of the table, Anders turned to Pilgrim.

'Charlotte, I think a drink would be good?'

Barrett contained his surprise. Had he just seen, what was essentially, a technology firm company exec treating the city's -- possible even the country's -- most senior government official like a butler? Barrett was apparently alone in this conclusion, however, as Pilgrim subserviently responded, walking immediately across to the nearby drinks caddy, preparing glasses, and looking across at Barrett expectantly for his order.

'I'm...fine, thank you.' Barrett declared, finding the whole episode mildly ironical that he was declining a drink from his most elevated boss, on the grounds that he was on duty. Anders solemnly peered at Barrett as his hand reached out to accept his own whisky and water. Anders began with a question.

'A man in your profession will, no doubt, be wondering why we...' waving a regal hand towards Pilgrim, '...have summoned you here?' Barrett nodded.

'Well, yes sir. There were a few raised eyebrows at the Department, to put it mildly.' Barrett replied cordially.

Anders chuckled slightly.

'Yes, I imagine there have been.' His face changed, to a serious expression. 'However, and I cannot stress this enough, what we are about to discuss with you is classified at the very highest level; do you understand?'

So how is it you have that kind of clearance? Barrett's inner voice asked.

'Of course, sir.'

Anders smiled. Pilgrim, having prepared her own drink, walked back to Anders' side.

'I think you may change your mind about that drink, my friend, once you know why you're here.' Anders smiled; Pilgrim smiled. The two officials chinked their glasses together. 'You see, well to put it to you succinctly, we would like you to save humankind.'

Northern France, September 6th, 1917

Midday

Seventeen times he'd saluted before he'd made it to B-Company's staff office. Three red caps, a senior officer, and lots and lots of parading soldiers: some marching -- at the double -- most running, he noticed. He smiled to himself remembering that, not long ago, he'd worried how authentic his salute looked, wondering whether it would pass scrutiny. It was clear he was going to have plenty of practise perfecting it. The staff office had the same grubby appearance as many of the 'buildings' he'd walked past on his way from the Mess. The front had a covered wooden veranda of duckboards, a style that reminded him of a saloon from the Wild West. Outside the entrance door, a chalkboard was fixed to the wall, showing Company staff names, starting with Major Davenport at the top, and descending in rank order. Each name had a tile hanging from a peg, two faced, showing in or out. Davenport's showed 'in'; the name below, Captain Renton -- who would be Barrett's own immediate commanding officer -- showed as being 'out'. Taking a deep breath, he turned the doorknob, and walked in.

Immediately inside he found himself in a shabby lobby, single doors to the left and right. In front, a desk, piled high with precariously slanting towers of paper. Over the top of these, a meek-looking face peered, at the sound of Barrett's entrance.

'Good afternoon, sir,' said the voice. 'Can I help you?'

Barrett approached the table, opening his top left breast pocket to extract his drafting paperwork.

'First Lieutenant Barrett, Royal Artillery.' He said no more. He'd remembered his earlier blunder of offering too much information, especially to lower ranks. He simply handed the docket across, glancing around the room, effecting a slightly aloof air of pseudo superiority. The private took the paper and disappeared for a moment, off into his underground lair of administration. Barrett had had plenty of time to run through what was coming. There would be no record of his posting, of course; in fact, no record of him at all. It would all be 'such a nuisance' that no-one had been informed of his arrival. It may even descend into a full-on obstreperous act, with Barrett feigning anger and suggesting that perhaps he ought to 'toddle off straight to the front, then'...or words to that effect. Wound up and ready to go, Barrett saw the private reappear, this time coming around the front of the desk.

'Very good, sir, thank you.' Handing the draft back to Barrett. 'If you'll follow me, sir.'

Barrett raised his eyebrows but said nothing. The private was already scurrying through the door on the left. The corridor beyond had several offices branching from it; they were heading for the end one, facing them; Barrett could make out the sign above the door: 'B-Comp. C.O.' The private knocked once and let himself through the door, partially pulling it closed behind him, subtly indicating that Barrett was not to follow. He could hear some low rumbling conversation as the adjutant explained Barrett's arrival. The private soon returned, a sheepish grin on his face; for a moment, Barrett wondered if he was going to be seen at all. A small voice called from beyond the door, inviting him to enter. He refitted his cap and went in.

Bringing himself smartly to attention, he saluted the major, sitting behind a large mahogany desk. In return, the major briefly stiffened upright, the indoors acknowledgement of a salute, then motioned for Barrett to take a seat. As he waited patiently, the major continued to shuffle papers around, seemingly preoccupied with something that had been interrupted. Barrett didn't believe it for a second; his mind returned to the last meeting he'd had with the Chief, back in the PD. The pantomime was the same now as it had been then: a broadcast that he was a very busy man. Barrett smiled inwardly to himself. He held master's degrees in both psychology and forensic investigative techniques; that, along with eighteen years in uniform, had taught him a few things about human behaviour, and whilst he waited for Davenport to engage him, he mentally ticked off a few likely scenarios. The most typical, and the most boring, Barrett thought, was the initial establishment of the major's *alpha male* superiority, a pretty superfluous gesture, since military rank structure already superimposed such an ordering. An alternative reason was that the major wanted to *appear* busy, when in fact he wasn't at all. This was a curious one, as such a display hardly seemed necessary, for the benefit of a junior officer. Yet another possibility, he supposed, was that this was an act taught at staff college, a fundamental part of...

'So, Lieutenant Barrett was it?' Davenport interrupted his thoughts, smiling at him broadly. His hands rested on the desk, fingers intertwined, presenting a demeanour that said, 'I'm ready for you now'. His voice was rather thin and reedy, and Barrett thought he noticed a slight eye twitch. Too early to tell, but potentially neurological. Other than this, he gave the impression of a fairly nondescript individual. Mid-forties, he estimated; a rather bland face, below Brylcreemed, side parted hair.

'Yes sir.' Barrett replied. He said no more, but instead waited, feeling it wiser that Davenport should lead the conversation. Davenport looked down at some paper before him, scrutinising what must have been a list of dispatches.

'No notice of your posting has been received at this end...' He glanced back up at Barrett, the smile still glued in place. '...but we are very much used to that here.'

Just then, the sound of distant gunfire was heard, somewhere off to Barrett's left. The major shook his head reassuringly, as he misinterpreted Barrett's surprise for anxiousness.

'Target practice at the range; no need to fret.' The major said, consolingly.

Barrett rebuked himself for showing a reaction. He had, of course, known that he would hear a lot of this: in this place, at this time. Yet it had still surprised him. Barrett pondered the major's words.

...no need to fret...? An odd turn of phrase.

Two thoughts flashed through his mind. The first related to his *supposed* reason for being here, in this particular camp. An important requirement for the operation had been that he needed a plausible back story. His had been conveniently constructed around an injury he'd sustained several years earlier: a stabbing wound to the right shoulder, which still plagued him with a nagging ache most days. This, easily verifiable, injury had handily doubled -- for this mission -- as a 'Blighty ticket': a wound serious enough to evacuate a man home to Britain, away from the war. Now, with the injury 'nicely healed', the story was that he was being slowly processed back to the line, via Étaples training camp, to assist his 'working up' preparation. The details of this had been expertly woven into the draft document, complete with a faux 'fit for duty' validation stamp.

His second thought was that this back story may not be necessary after all. Davenport's odd words seemed to suggest that he had already concluded Barrett's reason for being here: he had the lieutenant pegged as a coward. Barrett knew, from his research, that establishments like Étaples had often acted as convenient assignments for those laying low, hiding from the carnage. Davenport continued.

'I suggest you get settled in first. Simmons will show you around and introduce you to the men.' He paused for a moment, the smile suddenly absent. He seemed to be searching for the right words. When he did continue, Barrett thought he witnessed a momentary disdain, a slight curl of the lip, as if in response to a sudden, disagreeable smell.

'Your C.O., Captain Renton, is out at the moment; I will leave it to him to govern how you are to be employed.' He fixed Barrett with a steely glare, placing his hands, palms down, on the desk.

'Remember our purpose here lieutenant; we are preparing these men not just for combat, but to survive. You may have heard things about this establishment; some of these things are true...' He eased back in his chair '...and some, I would like to think, aren't.'

Barrett recognised in the man a masked desire to say more, but it was far too early to press him, and, more importantly, it was not part of his mission to pry into things of that nature.

'This is no holiday camp, Barrett...' Davenport continued, '...not for the soldiers heading up the line, nor for us. We have a task here that is as important as that happening a few miles away...' He nodded towards the window, as if the front lines were just beyond the glass. '...don't forget that.' Davenport stood up from behind his desk. The arrival interview was over. He offered Barrett a handshake.

'So, welcome to Étaples, lieutenant. If you have any problems, use the chain of command in the first instance, of course; but, should you wish to see me...directly...' he paused again, holding the handshake, looking into Barrett's eyes with an expression difficult to interpret, '...do not hesitate.' Eventually letting go, Barrett took a step backward, repeating the earlier routine of attention and salute, but as he walked back into the corridor, Davenport's words remained, like an echo.

London, April 10th, 2142

14:00 Hrs

Barrett eased himself back into his chair, grinning good naturedly. Anders and Pilgrim continued to smile, refraining from speaking, waiting. Eventually, Barrett filled in the silence.

'That's good. Saving humankind...I like it. Well, all this time, I knew I had a higher purpose.' Barrett went along with the joke. 'Can I expect a raise?' He chuckled.

Pilgrim glanced across at Anders with a knowing look. This was to be expected, her expression seemed to say. She tipped back her glass and drained the contents. Rising to her feet, she addressed Barrett.

'Well, I'll be in the next room. A pleasure meeting you Barrett; we'll talk further.' And with that, she exited through a rear door. Anders' stare had not altered; still smiling, his eyes had not veered from Barrett's once. After what seemed an age, he looked down at his own glass and swirled the contents, like a connoisseur admiring a goblet of cognac.

'Of course, this seems incredible to you, I completely understand, but believe me DI Barrett, I am in earnest.' Touching his temple, he began speaking again, but this time, not to Barrett. 'Daisy, could you transfer presentation suite control to me please.' Glancing back at Barrett, he smiled, pointing to his head. 'Integrated interfaces. It's not unlike your handheld consoles, but far more convenient.' Anders explained.

Barrett swivelled in his chair as a projector unit descended from the ceiling and began to display a screen in mid-air over the conference table. Anders rose from his seat and, tapping his index finger onto the ball of the same hand, a holographic image of, what appeared to be, some kind of remote control, materialised, hovering above his hand. He looked back at Barrett.

'You are right to be incredulous. Obviously, I need to persuade you.' He held a hand up to Barrett. 'Now, you are going to be fed a great deal of information, DI Barrett. Please, you must feel free to stop me at any time; it is of vital importance that you understand...everything.'

Barrett thought that the executive spoke like a kindly tour guide, an impression he knew must be an act. There was no way a person could reach the top of such a corporation like Horizon without having a killer streak, when required. Anders applied two more touches of his hand and a visual representation of the Earth came into view over the table. As Barrett watched, Anders began his address – *how many rehearsals has this taken,* he wondered fleetingly.

'As you know, Horizon, along with several other partner companies around the world, have been working tirelessly to try to repair this dying planet of ours. Its demise was once thought to be irreversible and, for those who tragically find themselves living outside of city barrier zones, that is a very understandable viewpoint.' He paused to give Barrett a hard yet sympathetic look. 'I know your background, DI Barrett. I am, of course, very aware of the death of your wife. You have my heartfelt condolences.' Barrett nodded an acknowledgement of Anders' respectful comment.

Someone has done their homework, he thought briefly.

Another touch of the hand and the hovering image changed to show expanding circles of shaded colour emanating from various points on the 'globe'. The circles apparently signified the historical spread of climate changing, emission hot spots, and Barrett could clearly see their origins: typically, areas of huge population growth - cities and large towns; however, very quickly, the animated circles began to overlap each other, their doubling becoming darker in colour. Anders' narration continued.

'We all know, that for a time, nation states fought a losing battle to try to organise a...shall we call it... a united front...such as it was.'

Barrett thought back to all the history books he'd read on the subject. How each of them had recorded the pitiful attempts made in the early millennium, all ultimately moot due to the blinkered greed of individuals. Barrett recalled a memorable analogy, someone had written, that had always stuck with him: Saving the planet (back then) was analogous to bailing out a sinking boat with a thimble, unaware of the fact that the boat was on fire!

'Rising temperatures and melting ice floes led to mass migration, starvation and conflict, virtually everywhere. By 2070 -- that watershed year so important to our history -- people all around the world lost faith with their governments. Mass revolts led to wide scale civil and social unrest: revolutions followed, coup d'états and swing governments, all trying desperately, but ultimately forlornly, to restore order.'

Barrett knew all of this. He was eager for Anders to reach the point, but it was also clear to him that this build-up was somehow necessary for what was to come. The animation changed again, this time showing the bright and garish emblem of Horizon: a vivid four-leaf clover.

'Horizon's motif of the four-leaf clover, as everyone hopefully knows, represents a rebirth and growth of a bright new future; however, significantly, the four-leaf element also identifies how we, as a species, will need a healthy dose of luck to be successful in our endeavours. The early forefathers of Horizon knew that for humanity to be saved, like the Ark story of old, some would go into the boat, while others would have to be sacrificed.'

Barrett bit down hard on his bottom lip. This ecclesiastical sermon was starting to annoy him. The man had stated that he knew of Barrett's past, so *please, cut to the chase...I've got the fucking T-shirt already.* Anders went on, oblivious to Barrett's growing impatience.

'Horizon's beneficence could only ever be extended so far...'

Yes, Barrett mused, the 'beneficence' was granted provided you were an engineer, health professional, educationalist (*the right ones*); basically, anyone that was deemed useful to the new utopia. Again, Barrett knew this; he also knew that it was an incredibly elitist, heavily biased selection process. To have been born and raised in the right place was a disgusting fact of life.

Was this the luck the clover represented?

Yet, over the years, Barrett had come to terms with this inequality; he had to, there was absolutely no point in lamenting in a pool of survivor guilt.

'...and gargantuan efforts have never ceased to bring us back from the brink. The cities of London, Birmingham, Manchester and Edinburgh stand as testament to these efforts, as do many other cities around the world...'

Jesus.

'...but it hasn't been enough.'

At last. The crux?

'Trust me when I say, that Horizon has investigated so many solutions, more than you perhaps have the imagination for, DI Barrett.'

And yet.

Anders touched his palm again and the globe vanished, replaced by a long line, stretching across the wide expanse of the boardroom. The only visible feature was a spot, roughly midway along the line, located just above Barrett's head. It was labelled with the present year, 2142.

'What is your understanding of time travel, DI Barrett?' Anders had sat down, after pouring himself another large Scotch. Barrett rubbed the shadow of stubble that was starting to grow over his jaw, trying to pre-empt what he thought was coming from the implied question.

'Well, I have plenty of sci-fi movies that have all had a stab at it, sir.' He shot a no-nonsense stare at Anders. 'Did they get it right? Is that what you're about to tell me?'

Anders smiled; he was clearly enjoying his performance.

'Well, yes...and no, actually. You see, popular fiction has often posited notions that were, well, by chance, loosely based on fact.' For a moment, his smile faded as he appeared to remember something less than pleasant. 'After 2070, Horizon, and companies like them, ploughed countless trillions into research and development of all kinds. It did not take our scientists long to realise that the world, as we then knew it, was, indeed, impossible to save. With so many people to heat, feed, provide power for, let alone the quality of the air, becoming more and more choked with harmful particulates, and all of this, combined with the other side of the coin: a rapidly dwindling quantity of resource. No amount of analysis could come up with a solution, based on the levels of technological know-how we had back then.' Anders stared down into his lap with an almost theatrical look of woe. 'In short, DI Barrett, in lieu of the feasible and the realistic, Horizon instructed its best people to begin looking into the bizarre and the fantastic. Absolutely nothing was off the table.' Anders face had lit up again.

'In the thirty years from 2070 to the turn of the century, the vast majority of our funding was funnelled into the concept of temporal mechanics. The original notion, set by one of our greatest visionaries, Lawrence Cooper, concluded that if we could not do much about our present, was there some way that we could prevent such a condition from happening in the first place...?'

Barrett could no longer contain himself, he spurted out an interruption.

'What do you mean? How would that even be possible? I mean, where would the start of the problem be? The Industrial Revolution? What?'

Anders, with a fatherly smile, moved his hands up and down, palms facing downwards, the international body language for 'be calm.'

'I understand your frustration, and we could spend the next hour discussing the theories, but there is no need to...you see, in exploring this possibility, it was found that such a proposal was impossible to achieve.' Anders stood up again before continuing. 'In looking for this possible solution, we discovered that, contrary to all the popular imaginings, time does not work that way.' Walking around the head of the table, Anders pointed at Barrett.
'Think back to your library of 'sci-fi movies'...tell me, how often does the concept of multiple universes appear, as a common trope?' Before Barrett could consider, Anders went on; he was in full show-and-tell mode now, positively buoyant with himself. 'On this occasion, DI Barrett, it appears that they *did* get it right. Multiple universes are not fiction, at all; they do exist. In fact, it was our discovery of their existence which prevented us, for the most part anyway, from going back and 'fixing' the past, as we'd intended.'

Stop. Barrett's mind cried out in confused silence. I've had it with this. He glanced at the glass in Anders' hand.

'Do you think I could get that drink now, please?'

Northern France, September 6th, 1917

13:30 hrs

Private Simmons, B-company's adjutant -- the meek administrator who had shown Barrett in to see the major -- was now walking slightly ahead of the lieutenant, pointing out areas of interest, as the two went on a familiarisation tour of the camp. Simmons wore a soft fabric, blue armband, signifying his duties as a member of staff.

'It keeps me out of 'arm's way with the canaries.' He informed Barrett as they set off.

'Exactly what is a canary?' asked Barrett, having some recollection that they were part of the disciplinary staff. Simmons glanced at Barrett with a look that seemed to question the officer's motives for asking. Barrett softened his expression as much as he could, hoping to tempt the young lad to speak his mind.

'Well sir, I'll let you be the judge of that.' Clearly, Simmons had decided it was not worth the risk of getting caught out. Barrett persisted, with an amenable tone.

'Come now, Simmons, I need to know the men I am going to be working with.' He winked at the private conspiratorially. 'You won't know this, but I have been out of it for some time. Copped a 'Blighty' two years ago; surely the army has not changed all that much, while I've been away.'

The private, emboldened a little by being taken into the confidence of the officer, ventured his take on the matter.

'Well sir, it's like this: they aren't really reg'lar soldiers, if you take my meaning.' Barrett raised an eyebrow to register that he didn't. Simmons went on. 'They's mostly from glass 'ouses, I mean, prisons...from civvy street, sir.' He looked around himself furtively as he spoke, as if a canary might be right behind him, listening. 'They was brought in for the training...of the men, sir.' Then, after a short thought, 'I suppose a lot of the old drill instructors had already bought it.' He stopped talking, as if what he had said was explanation enough. Barrett played ignorant.

'So, experienced with dealing with men then? I daresay there's no trouble, with them on hand?'

Simmons scoffed involuntarily, then went quiet. It was obvious that he felt he'd already said too much. Barrett pushed again, recognising the signs that this pool of information was about to run dry.

'Go on, Simmons, you can't leave it there. Do you mean that discipline is lacking here?' Simmons stopped walking and turned to face Barrett, his face expressing something between anger and fear.

53

'No sir, I don't mean that. Not at all. If anything, there is too much discipline. Though I never said that. Now if you'll pardon me, sir.' He ended the conversation with a clear air of finality. Barrett persisted no more. In truth, Barrett knew a little of what Simmons meant from the, albeit sparse, documentation regarding what he knew to be brewing. But, like the good historian he considered himself to be, he also knew that what was written often differed a great deal from what turned out to be real.

Just then, a squad of men came jogging past: at least forty, all wearing full kit and carrying their Lee Enfield rifles high above their heads. To a man, they looked fit to drop. Their breathing was hoarse and laboured, their faces, pouring sweat. As they passed, Barrett noticed their boots were coated with wet sand and he could see the tide mark halfway up their puttees, indicating the depth they had obviously been wading through. From the other side of the group, a terrible noise could be heard; it sounded like the screaming of an animal. Barrett could make out the stiff, slashed peak of a service dress cap bouncing up and down on the far side of the men. He could also see, through the ranks, that the wearer of the slashed peak had a different colour arm band to the one Simmons wore; it was a yellow arm band – a canary. The convoy moved away, constantly barracked by the canary's screeches. Over his shoulder, Simmons provided commentary.

'That's one of our groups, sir. And that's Cpl Tomkinson; he's been taking them on the 'Canary Run', down to the beach and back.' Barrett looked at his watch, it was just after two in the afternoon.

'What time does that begin?' He enquired. Simmons, shrugged.

'They would have gone out after morning muster, around six, give or take.' He said nonchalantly.

No wonder they looked exhausted, Barrett thought.

'That's a rough day then, the Canary Run?' he asked. Simmons shook his head.

'It's not over yet, sir. They'll be in the Bull Ring -- our parade ground -- for another two hours yet, doing drill.' Simmons saw the shocked look on Barrett's face. 'Then it'll be tea.' He said quickly, as if the notion of some hot food would somehow make up for a full day of relentless physical training. They walked on, following the route the men had taken.

As they continued, the din of marching boots, the metallic slap of rifles and the guttural cries of 'left turn, right turn, quick march', could be clearly heard, ahead. Barrett realised he was about to see the 'Bull Ring', firsthand. The parade ground was a huge square surrounded on all sides by the huts and tents of the encampment. There had to be at least five hundred men marching this way and that, and Barrett estimated the 'ring' could probably accommodate at least the same number again. As they approached, he noticed men standing around at the Ring's perimeter fence; they appeared to be hatless, as if spectating. This didn't seem likely, and Barrett was about to ask Simmons what was going on when he stopped himself. There was something odd in the way the men were standing. For one thing, they were not moving, as people tend to do when they are loitering. They were stock still. As they continued to close the distance, Barrett saw the reason for their immobility. They had been tied to the fences. Those closest to him, he could see, were standing, bolt upright, unable to adopt a different position due to the bindings that snaked around them, fastening their hands behind their backs, then secured tightly to the fence post. One man, however, had slumped down. He looked, at this distance, to be unconscious, but Barrett could see how the ropes were pulling his arms upwards, behind him, as his own weight threatened to wrench his arms out of his shoulders. Barrett started to pick up pace, his walk turning into a slow run. Simmons' voice rose in alarm as he realised what this odd officer might be about to do.

'Sir, what are you doing, sir?'

Barrett ignored him, his pace turning into a full run. As he neared, he realised the tied-up soldier was on the other side of the fence. Barrett would need to head for a break in the perimeter to get around to him. He could see two thicker posts forming an entry into the Ring and made directly for it. Simmons had been forgotten now; Barrett could see nothing but the plight of the man being punished. He passed through the gate posts, ignoring the two guards at the 'entrance' who snapped robotically to attention as he passed. In another ten seconds, he had reached the tied man. As suspected, he was out cold. Barrett grabbed his jacket with both hands, trying to lift him up. The soldier's dead weight made this difficult, and Barrett looked around for some assistance. He saw troubled looks from men marching by; some looks of pity, some of genuine fear. He was about to call for help when a loud shout cannoned across the square.

'That man, there!'

Barrett could see, from the corner of his eye, someone running towards him from the other side of the parade ground. He had some kind of stick, carried in one hand. He had to be a canary; Barrett guessed. He continued to try to get the soldier standing, though there was no rousing him. *He must be practically in a coma,* Barrett thought. He heard the shout again, nearer now, this time addressing someone else.

'You two, apprehend that man, at the double.'

Barrett sensed, rather than saw, two men, on either side rapidly approaching, then, suddenly, coming to an abrupt stop. The voice again, only some twenty metres away now.

'I said hold him, you lousy, useless scum.' The two accomplices were having second thoughts. Barrett glanced at one of them. They, being much closer than the canary, had recognised Barrett's rank and were frozen to the spot – unsure what to do. Barrett took the initiative.

'You two men take hold of him...' nodding towards the slumped soldier. '...lift him up until we can untie him.' The men stood for a second, risking a quick glance at each other, then did as they were instructed. As they hoisted the unconscious man, Barrett loosened his grip and took a step back, just as the canary finally arrived, behind him.

'What the bloody 'ell is going on here?' No longer a shout, but, dripping with foreboding.

Barrett turned towards the canary. He could see the man's face, bright crimson, sparking with animosity. Then, with a flash of recognition, the corporal brought his heels together, one arm tight to his side, the other tucking his 'yard stick' under his armpit. His expression had faltered for a split second as he assessed the situation. He looked Barrett up and down, then at the men awkwardly holding the bound soldier. Barrett could almost sense his thoughts, could see how quickly he was formulating a recovery. Barrett felt his advantage was temporary.

What was it they always said about the best form of defence?

'You there. Corporal...?' He effected an arch tone, hoping it would be enough to prevent any obstruction. The canary replied, a curled lip of defiance forming over his pencil-thin moustache.

'Corporal Smithers, B-Company training staff, sir; and may I ask who you are?' The manner in which he asked the question made Barrett suspect that his senior rank held no real significance to the man. Barrett would need to be bold.

'I am Lieutenant Barrett, as of this morning, also of B-Company. Now, I want you...' He pointed directly at Smithers' face, '...to supervise taking this man to the hospital.' The corporal glanced again at the unconscious soldier, then back to Barrett.

'I think not, sir. Army Field Punishment Number One had been authorised for all of these men, direct from the captain, sir, no exceptions.' A smirk was forming on the vile man's face. He reached into his trouser pocket, pulled out a gold watch on a chain and looked at it. 'He still has another fifteen minutes of this duty remaining.' He looked back into Barrett's eyes. '...sir'.

Barrett felt the warmth of blood as a flush of anger began to rise up through his neck, threatening to invade his cheeks. *He couldn't let this little bastard see that*, he thought to himself, grimly. Barrett had never served in a military outfit, but his years in the police bolstered his response.

'I think you misunderstand me, corporal, so try to listen this time.' The smirk on the canary's face instantly vanished; it was his turn to flush, adding a new shade of red to his already burgundy complexion. Barrett went on. 'I am issuing you with a *new* order, and you shall carry it out immediately. Take this man to the hospital and see that he is well looked after.'

That would have been enough, Barrett thought much later, but he wanted to put this bastard in his place; no, that's not quite true, he wanted to humiliate the little runt in front of those he was so obviously abusing, on a daily basis.

'And, let me be clear on one more matter. If you play that game with me again, I shall have you strung up here instead.'

Smithers looked ready to have an aneurism. His face had gone from deep red to a waxy, sick-looking white. The knuckles of his left hand, grasping the brass pommel of his yard stick, had gone a similar colour. Barrett noticed for the first time that a crowd of men, who had previously been marching, had stopped to watch the drama unfold. He saw one or two crack a grin, one or two whisper to the other. Out of the silence of the moment, the routine noise of the parade square began to slowly resume, not least due to the restoring efforts of a few canaries, rounding up the spectators. Barrett stood motionless, waiting, watching Smithers come to terms with his new reality. After what seemed an age, Smithers quietly addressed the two men holding the still senseless soldier.

'Untie him.' He looked around and selected two more troops at random. 'You two, go fetch a stretcher and help these men.'

A few minutes passed before they were prepared to move off. As they passed Barrett, Smithers looked at him with unbridled hatred; he looked as though he was about to utter some last-word comment, then felt better of it. Barrett looked around and found Simmons, waiting patiently at the perimeter gate. As he walked back towards the adjutant, he felt suddenly exhausted as the adrenaline subsided; he knew the feeling, had felt it often enough, but, this time, he couldn't help think that he'd really screwed up.

London, April 10th, 2142

15:30 hrs

The warmth of the alcohol spread throughout Barrett's throat and down into his chest. He relished how the liquor brought small tears to his eyes as the Scotch took a bite out of him. He had not tasted whisky for several years. Operating distilleries were probably very few in number, he reckoned. He knew the Glenkinchie plant still existed, on the outskirts of Edinburgh, but could not be sure as to others. For certain, the much-reduced supply would have driven up the price of the commodity, far higher than a mere DI could justifiably afford, at any rate. Anders had left the room, leaving Barrett to enjoy the booze in solitude. He had already had enough of this history lesson-cum-sci-fi babble. And yet, his presence here, in such vaunted company, could only signify that it had to be legit. There were certainly easier, less sophisticated ways to play a practical joke.

The rear door at the back of the room swung open and Anders strode back in, oddly, carrying an umbrella. Were they about to take a stroll? The brolly looked quite antiquated, and Barrett fleetingly wondered if it was a family heirloom. Certainly, few people used them these days, even though the rain almost never stopped. Barrett opened it up and positioned it so that its wooden, hockey stick-style handle touched the floor. He held it by the short, stubby tip that jutted up from the centre of the canopy.

'Please indulge me a simple demonstration, DI Barrett. I have found that this sometimes helps to conceptualise things.' He dipped his index finger into his whisky glass, then held it, hovering over the brolly tip. Barrett could see the whisky coalescing into a droplet on his outstretched finger, welling up, ready to fall.

'Consider this drop of whisky as an event that you or I create, right here, right now, in our present lives, our...present universe, if you will.'

The droplet eventually fell from Anders' finger, and the two men watched it initially dribble down the tip of the brolly, then down onto the fabric canopy. For a moment, the droplet didn't move further, just held its position, but then, with increasing speed, it rolled down the convex shape of the opened umbrella, leaving a thin, visible trail in its wake.

'Now, think about all the different paths that droplet *could* have taken, down this umbrella; the different routes it could have gone, following, perhaps, imperfections in the fabric.' He looked up at Barrett, giving a mildly condescending smile, like a father showing his son some nugget of wisdom.

'I need you to imagine that all those different routes all represent the vast number of universes that run, forever parallel, to our own. Though I actually created this event, its aftermath can be felt in only one of any number of pathways; that is to say, any number of universes. Now, just like our little droplet here, we cannot simply choose to go *into* any of these alternate timelines at will...' He winked at Barrett. '...yet.

'But...and this is the point of this rather simplistic analogy, and the nub of the whole space-time question...due to the sheer incalculable number of possible routes open - from that single starting point, that...creation of an event, in time and space - the notion that a change, *prior to the event,* could importantly affect its future, is virtually impossible.' Anders clicked his fingers, dramatically. 'This knocks out the whole chaos theory, butterfly effect and so on...' He looked at Barrett to make sure he was following.

Barrett wasn't following.

Admittedly, he'd heard something about these theories: that small, seemingly imperceptible changes *now* can have momentous effects *later*. At this moment, however, he simply shrugged – much to the apparent annoyance of Anders, who was becoming frustrated trying to make the detective understand.

'There have been many concepts that suppose, falsely, I might add, that everything is connected with an intrinsic cause and effect linearity. This theory was developed into the idea of determinism. For example, the butterfly...you will no doubt remember such a creature from biology lessons? Well, the butterfly was chosen as an example since, being so incredibly delicate and lightweight, you may think it would have no causal bearing on anything. But -- so the theory goes -- although so seemingly trivial, the butterfly flaps its wings, say, over there...' Pointing to a desk in the corner. '...and, then, later, as a result, a typhoon develops in, oh I don't know, Beijing!' Anders looked imploringly at Barrett for confirmation that he understood, his patience seemingly growing thin.

Barrett slowly nodded an affirmative.

'My point here, DI Barrett, is that, for the most part, timelines *cannot* just be reset in the way fiction has led us to imagine...well, not for the most part. In other words, it is just impossible, I am afraid, to simply go back in time and...well, dis-invent the steam engine.'

Anders reached for Barrett's empty glass, not enquiring if he wanted another. Barrett ventured what he hoped was an encouraging contribution.

'What was always referred to as, a temporal paradox...?' He asked, remembering the phrase from more than one time-travel movie. Anders grinned in reply.

'Yes...Exactly! This is what our more recent discoveries have proved to be incorrect.' The executive beamed, satisfied that Barrett was back on the same page. 'But the findings determine that, in fact, very little seems to disturb the direction of events. Time, it appears, is very stable.' Anders spread his palms wide in a gesture that seemed to suggest he had reached the end of his explanation. Barrett, sat back, running the fingers of both hands through his hair. He had so many questions. Anders, sensing his curiosity, continued on, as he walked back to the drinks caddy.

'Some years ago, twenty-six to be exact, the scientific team found that, even though we found it impossible to go back and make changes that could affect our own human trajectory...due to the relative stability of our timeline...it was still possible for us to at least look ahead into our future.' Barrett suddenly sat forward.

'We cannot see specifics, events of any recognisable nature, but we *can* determine the presence of human activity, or at least strong indicators of it.' Another two generous splashes of single malt went into the glasses.

'How far forward is it possible to see?' Barrett asked. Anders rocked one of his hands, like a set of scales, struggling to balance.

'Estimates vary. The odd thing is, we can look backwards with an extremely accurate level of sensitivity, yet forwards is...well, hazy. I don't pretend to fully understand all the intricacies of why this is so, suffice to say that the bottom line appears to be that, since the future hasn't happened yet, it is more difficult to visualise.' This had a reasonable logic, Barrett thought, as he took another swallow of liquor.

'Our best evaluations give us a forward view of around five to six hundred years.' At this, Anders looked back at his right palm; two presses of his fingers brought a second point into view on the floating holographic line; this one read 2750. Barrett had completely forgotten the display was there. 'For a long time, monitoring this future gradually garnered more and more results; we were starting to see some...' Anders looked up to the ceiling, searching for the right word. '...granularity.' He looked back at Barrett again. 'For instance, large scale events became discernible. There is, in about two hundred years from now, evidence that the Earth gets hit by a meteorite.' He let that sink in for a second before continuing.

'Importantly, we could see *continued* human activity.' Looking into Barrett's eyes, Anders' own seemed to be welling up with tears. 'You see the importance of this, DI Barrett; for so long we had thought that our global antipathy would see the end of us, that all we could see was our species, spiralling down the toilet bowl. Now...suddenly...we had some hope. Human involvement had been identified, far past even that meteor impact. Despite how bleak our present still is, we had the knowledge that we could ultimately find our way out of all this.' Despite, Anders' joyous overtones, Barrett, ever the policeman, returned to the harsh, bottom line.

'Sir, you said you needed me to...' Barrett used the two-finger quotation sign. '...save humankind. So, I am guessing there is something wrong with this picture you are painting.'

Anders' reverie came to an end. The glint in his eyes faded, replaced by a dull stare.

'Indeed.' He said simply.

Northern France, September 6th, 1917

17:15 hrs

The door exploded inwards, swinging on its hinges so violently that it struck the wall, leaving a dent as the knob made an impact. Barrett, who had been sat behind his desk, leapt to his feet, feigning shock. The truth was that he'd *heard* his C.O.'s arrival, rampaging into the building like a rutting elephant. He had also expected an outrage, after the scene he'd created at the Bull Ring. What he hadn't expected was the sheer ferocity of the entrance, at least, not from an 'officer and gentleman'. There was nothing gentle about this man. He filled the doorway, all two metres of him, his scalp just brushing the inside of the frame. When he spoke, his voice was initially quite low, despite the violent ingress, and Barrett detected a mild Scottish burr that somehow added a dangerous edge to his words.

'Who the *fuck* do you think you are?'

The obscenity rocked Barrett more than the strongman act; for some odd reason he had not imagined he would hear such words, *not here, not now.* Barrett stood to attention, waiting in silence, not falling for the trap of attempting to answer what was obviously a rhetorical question. Since coming back to the staff rooms, he had replayed the earlier episode through his mind, several times.

What the hell was I thinking? Was the common question that had kept springing into his mind. He had a job to do, and publicly administering twenty-second century justice had never been part of it. His forensic evaluation, after due consideration, was that he'd acted like an arsehole, and now he had to get back on task as soon as possible, which meant taking an almighty bollocking for starters. Captain Alistair Renton walked into the room, leaving the door wide open behind him.

Oh yes, Barrett thought, *he wanted everyone to hear this.*

He looked more like a heavyweight boxer than a captain in the British Army. His huge hands hung down by his sides as he circled around in front of the desk, dominating the room like a uniformed Silverback Gorilla, as if establishing some animalistic, territorial ground rules.

'Well, Lieutenant Barrett of the Royal fucking Artillery, you have certainly had yourself a busy first day, haven't you?' He came around the desk, to within a few centimetres of Barrett, standing above him, intimidating with his size, his voice, rising in volume with every word. Barrett found himself staring at the big man's chest. 'Not only did we have no fucking clue you were coming, but you seem to have spared no time in countermanding my fucking orders, creating a fucking spectacle in the Ring, and instigating a potentially dangerous situation by dressing down one of my best fucking staff, in front of the goons!' The last few words were accompanied by globs of spittle, raining down on Barrett's head. At this proximity, he also found himself being engulfed by the big man's foul-smelling breath, *spicy sausage and red wine?*

Renton took a pace back and swivelled on one heel, looking out of the window, intensity lessening, slightly.

'I understand that you have been wallowing around in Suburbia, before coming back here, perhaps hoping you'd done your bit for King and country...and that, perchance, you wouldn't need to return? But let me educate you on that score, laddie: every soldier in this bloody army is needed...' He waved a hand towards the window, '...all of those bloody malingerers...out there...are needed, if we are to have any chance of stopping the Hun from winning this thing.' He turned back to Barrett with a renewed aggression. 'All they need is a fucking bleeding heart like you to show them a bit of T, L, fucking C and we'll be buggered! Just like those bastard Frogs, throwing in the towel, left and right.' He seemed to stop for a moment, gathering himself. He went back to the window and stood, looking out, hands resting on his hips, apparently deep in thought. Eventually, he turned back into the room, eyes staring into Barrett's, his tone returning to a more conversational level.

'What you need to understand, and quick, is that we are sitting on a powder keg here. Those men don't want to go up the bloody line...you'd have to be bloody barmy to want that...but, without discipline, without a fucking stick up their arse, they're not going to go; it's as simple as that.' He slowly walked towards Barrett again. Coming closer, his voice dropped in volume, becoming more confidential. 'So, when you come along and cut one of them down from field punishment, what message does that send?'

His eyes bored into Barrett's, looking for acceptance of his argument. Barrett understood the line of reasoning. He admitted to himself he had no idea what kept men moving forward, into the machine gun fire, into certain bloody slaughter. Of course, he'd read as much as he could about the war, the battles, the sheer carnage, but he couldn't grasp it, not really. How could he? He acknowledged that there was some logic in what Renton said, but, with the benefit of hindsight, he knew that men could also only take so much. And this hindsight also told him that the medicine -- Renton and his men were administering -- was soon going to be spat out. Despite all this, Barrett knew what he had to say.

'I'm sorry, sir. I guess I just didn't understand the bigger picture. It won't happen again.'

Renton maintained a steady stare for what seemed like an age, scanning Barrett's face for evidence of sincerity. Eventually, his expression began to soften; he offered a thin smile. Walking over to Barrett, he patted him on the shoulder with a large shovel-like hand.

'You're not the first, laddie.' He conceded ruefully.

He pulled out a chair, motioning for Barrett to do the same. Barrett quietly breathed out. Hopefully, the bashful act had repaired some of the damage he'd brought on himself. Renton's temper seemed to have subsided as quickly as it had come, and as the big captain looked Barrett in the eye once again, he recognised a friendlier glimmer.

'Simmons tells me you caught a Blighty wound?'

Chalk that one up Barrett thought, *Simmons didn't waste any time.* Barrett coughed in faux modesty.

'Not much to tell, sir. I took a bullet in the shoulder at the Somme.' He paused and looked down into his lap, feeling more than a little fraudulent. 'We lost a lot of good men.' He looked up to see Renton nodding solemnly. Sitting forward, the captain unbuttoned a breast pocket and took out a hip flask. Unscrewing the lid, he took a quick swig, and passed it across to Barrett.

'Similar story, laddie.' Renton said, as Barrett took the flask. 'I was there at the beginning...Mons.' He waited for Barrett to accept his offer. Barrett upended the flask, tasting the sharp sting of the whisky. It seemed that their mutual wounds -- obtained 'in action' -- might form the basis for a common bond.

Maybe something I can work with? Barrett pondered, handing back the flask, nodding his thanks. Renton continued.

'You and I, we know what it means to come to terms with the man upstairs...' he looked upwards briefly, then back to Barrett. 'But, it's a different story now...' He looked around the room '...here.' He paused, staring dolefully at the walls; his thoughts, somewhere else. Barrett detected a tone in his voice, *was he ashamed?* Renton seemed to want to say more, but thought better of it, and brusquely stood up.

'Right. I think we understand one another.' Pocketing the flask, he turned for the door. Walking out, leaving the door open, he called back over his shoulder.

'Your Étaples education starts tomorrow, lieutenant. See you in the Mess.'

London, April 10th, 2142

16:00 hrs

Anders sat down again at the conference table, with a heavy slump.

'Just over twelve years ago, our monitoring efforts revealed an incredibly disturbing find. As I said before, our research -- our ability -- to see the future time stream, showed plenty of human interaction, at least as far forward as the date you see up there.' Pointing to the 2750 spot on the hologram above the table. 'And then, inexplicably, the computers started kicking out screen after screen of spurious data. It took us quite a time to decipher it.' He sighed. 'Eventually we did, of course, though the results were confusing at first, and certainly contrary to our earlier findings. The new data shows that at around the year 2488, human activity...stops.'

Barrett said nothing, waiting for Anders to go on.

'Of course, such a discovery needed confirmation. Thus, began a very long phase of round the clock analysis, multi-level sampling; endless discussion; alternative theories being bandied around; computer modelling, anything...everything...trying to fathom what had gone wrong. It took five long years, and the combined efforts of our greatest scientific minds, and all our resources...but, finally, we had an answer.'

Once again, Anders glanced down at his hand; another touch, this time, thumb to ring finger. Up above, the holographic timeline began to faintly skip up and down at various points along its length. Barrett wondered for a moment whether the program was glitching. It had a sporadic effect, like it was about to splutter out. Anders, oblivious to the effect, carried on.

'It was found, the deeper our analysis went, that timelines are somehow disturbed now and again – hence these little blips you see represented here. We genuinely do not know exactly how these disturbances occur, but we are now quite certain as to *why* they occur. You will recall that we had a much more accurate sense of what had taken place in the past, by comparison to what we can see in the future?' Barrett nodded. 'Well, it appears that, at the exact moment the timeline changed for us, 2488, one of these disturbances -- what our scientists have labelled as 'ripples' -- was detected at a date in our past.' Anders paused and stared into Barrett's eyes. Barrett screwed his face up in confusion.

'So...you're saying that something that has happened in the past has affected our future?' He rubbed his forehead. 'I'm sorry, sir, forgive me, but I thought you said that time didn't work like that...that the whole butterfly, chaos thing was disproven?' Anders grinned like a proud parent.

'Yes, yes, that is correct DI Barrett.' He clapped his hands together. 'I am so happy you understand.' Sensing Barrett's growing frustration, however, he moved on quickly. 'You are completely right; we *have* disproven it. As I said, the sheer uncountable number of universes running parallel to ours completely smooths out that probability.'

'But...?' Barrett said, willing Anders to bottom line it.

'These discovered ripples change the whole ball game. As I said, they happen sporadically, and we don't really understand their initiation; but, what we do know about them is that they are anomalies...mistakes... errors in the time stream and, crucially, for some reason that we do not understood at all, they *do* change the timeline...' Anders sat back with a huge sigh.

Barrett stood and began to slowly walk around the table, a behaviour that he would never have done ordinarily in such a setting, in such company; so focused, however, so engrossed was he, that it never occurred to him.

'So, this particular ripple...can you see what it is?' Barrett asked.

Anders nodded excitedly.

'Yes.'

'And it's some kind of mistake, you say? It...what...should never have happened?'

'That's right.'

Barrett stopped, turned and placed both palms face down on the table. His look expressed the question that he did not need to ask. Anders dropped the bomb.

'DI Barrett, before I say anything further, I want you to understand that in the last three decades we have discovered a positive future for our planet, one we could not have dreamed to have thought possible, even with our best efforts. But then, almost laughably, like some great cosmic joke, we get to see our own untimely demise. It's almost farcical. To have glimpsed a way out of this, human-induced, environmental nightmare, and then? Out of the frying pan, into the fire.'

'Since knowledge of this ripple has come to light, it will be of no surprise to you that *all* of the global partners came together, in an effort to bring a solution to the table. Nothing, I mean absolutely nothing, has taken more priority than this; the financial costs outstrip everything we have ever done, including the city-wide environmental reconstructions we have carried out over the decades.'

Anders paused, jutting his chin out slightly; his expression seemed to show...was it pride? Barrett wondered.

'We are now, for the first time, supremely confident. After countless tests and trials, we have the information we need, we have the technological means at our disposal. We are ready to send a person back to this most crucial point in our history, to seek out and correct the anomaly...to correct the ripple.'

Barrett's knees suddenly felt weak; in that precise moment he realised why he had been brought here. *Jesus, was he going to faint?* Anders rose from his chair, so that both men were facing each other.

'DI Barrett, you are the person our computers, our analysis, our predictive algorithms, our evaluations have come up with...you are the person we need to send back and correct our future. You, DI Barrett, are the person history has selected to save humankind.'

Two hours later, back in his own apartment, Barrett practically collapsed into his couch. The mild fogginess, brought on by the whisky he was so unaccustomed to, was ebbing away, but his mouth had an unpleasantly parched feel, and he felt completely exhausted. He replayed the meeting back through his mind again, for perhaps the fiftieth time since leaving Horizon. He could not remember the chauffeur-driven journey back to his building; no way could he have driven his own vehicle – the booze had put him way over the top for any kind of safe, or legal, act.

After the *raisen d'etre* for his summons had been made clear, Anders had poured yet another shot for them both, followed by a bizarre downshift into small talk. The CEO wanted Barrett to go away and sleep on it. Such bombshells don't come every day, he'd said banally. What Barrett found both equally amusing and disturbing, was that the act of 'sleeping on it' was not a suggestion to mull it over, or to take time to come to a decision. The executive had made it pretty clear that Barrett *was* the man for this. No discussion; the computer had said so. The detail of the mission could come later; after all, they had over three hundred years to 'sleep on it'; no rush. Despite the traffic jam of thoughts trying to jump the queue into his mind, he closed his eyes, and in seconds, he was sleeping deeply.

Northern France, September 7th, 1917

07:30 hrs

Pulling the razor down his cheek, Barrett contemplated the day ahead. His head was still fuzzy from the three pints of beer he'd consumed the night before, in the bar. Conscious of Renton's parting words: 'see you in the Mess', he had wanted to ingratiate himself as much as possible after so narrowly avoiding disaster. However, despite his eagerness to please his new superior, Renton hadn't shown up. While waiting, Barrett had passed the time with two other officers, tentatively soaking up whatever intel he could. He couldn't believe how much alcohol these men could drink. As the night wore on, Barrett had, out of necessity, taken regular trips out through the Mess French doors, onto the patio, so as to pour the majority of his own ale into the ground. The other officers, it transpired, were from A and C companies, lieutenants both. The word was that B-Company had been running light for several weeks, with Captain Renton directly managing his own little band of canaries: Corporal Tomkinson, he of the screeching canary run detail; Smithers, of whom Barrett had already clashed with, and another man called Lyman, a skinny cockney, apparently renowned for his petty cruelty. Charming little team, Barrett thought. No other subalterns were employed - until he'd 'arrived', of course. Little was known of B-Company's C.O., Major Davenport. The rumour was, however, that there was no love lost between him and Renton; reason: unknown.

He rubbed a towel across his face and winced as he saw the damage the razor had wrought. After returning from the Bull Ring, he had gone to the commissary to purchase a few essentials. Fathoming the currency was straightforward enough, but he had never before used a blade razor, nor was he familiar with toothpaste and brush; removing stubble, and bacteria from the teeth, had long since dispensed with such barbaric implements. His face reflected his lack of competence and he grimaced as he counted at least ten dots of blood, starting to clot and crust.

After breakfast -- tea and scrambled eggs on toast, complete with some tiny, but sufficiently off-putting eggshell, thrown in for good measure -- Barrett made his way swiftly to the staff room. On the short walk he contemplated the date; *have I really only been here just over twenty-four hours?* He made a mental note of how long he had before things began to get truly interesting. He needed to assess the situation more closely than opportunity had presented, so far. He needed to understand who the major players would be in this mystery he'd been sent to solve. From the little he had seen thus far, he reckoned he'd have a reasonable chance to stay close to the action; but time was getting short.

Entering the staff building, he could hear Renton's deep tones; the sound suggested he was in good spirits and, from the accompanying laughter, it was apparent that others shared in the hilarity. Opening the canteen door, Barrett walked in to find the captain holding centre stage. Around him, his three stooges: Smithers, Tomkinson and a weasly little man Barrett assumed must be Lyman. All the NCOs were seated in a horseshoe pattern, smoking and guffawing at their leader. As Barrett closed the door, all stopped to look at him; the room, immediately silent. Over in the far corner, another man stood stirring a spoon in a mug of tea – *in the room, but not part of the room*, at least as it seemed to Barrett. Renton, momentarily pausing his delivery, addressed his entourage.

'Here we are lads, a full team again.' He nodded towards the tea-stirrer. 'Like buses; none at all, then two turn up together.'

This brought another broadside of guffaws from the corporals, worshiping the big captain, like fawning toadies around a schoolyard bully. Barrett looked back at the man in the corner, noticing the single pip on his epaulette – a second lieutenant - the most junior grade of commissioned officers, one rank below Barrett. Renton, enjoying the adulation, wrenched himself away and motioned for Barrett to join him, as he walked over to the other man.

'Barrett, this is Lieutenant Sumner, just arrived this morning to join our merry band.'

Sumner stood rather stiffly, waiting apprehensively, Barrett thought. Barrett offered his hand in greeting. Sumner warily shook it, the proverbial rabbit caught in headlights.

'How do you do, sir.' He said nervously, his voice barely audible. Thinking about his own reception the day before, Barrett was empathetic. He wondered what kind of pep talk Renton had already delivered. Rather a harsh one, judging from the visible meekness apparent.

'How do you do.' Barrett returned, and then, quickly, in an effort to put the man at ease: 'Call me Liam.' A tiny smile kinked the corner of Sumner's mouth, which Barrett read as: *Thank God, a human being.* Glancing briefly at the captain, then back to Barrett, Sumner gratefully offered a rejoinder.

'Lionel.'

Barrett judged Sumner to be perhaps ten years or so younger than himself, certainly no more than twenty-eight or nine. A little old to be a second lieutenant, perhaps, but Barrett thought he detected an uneasiness about him, that was more than simple first-day nerves. *Shell shock?* Before he could engage in small talk, Renton barraged in, waving a hand back at the seated hyenas.

'My merry men.'

Seemingly on cue, the three junior NCOs got up from their chairs. Stooges, yes; but, clearly knowing how to play the game when required. Renton went on.

'Smithers, you've met.' Smithers gave a respectful nod, fully compliant now in front of the 'big dog'. He cleared his throat with a slight cough.

'Sorry about the other day, sir. The captain has told us how you weren't fully aware of what 'appens 'ere.' He said, in a convincingly humble tone.

Yes, I'm sure he has. Barrett thought, but merely nodded in reply.

Next was Tomkinson. A tall, broad chested Geordie who looked to Barrett like a man who should really have a deep sonorous voice, rather than the high-pitched squeal he had heard the day before. Barrett, filling the void of silence enquired after the Canary Run he'd seen, asking if it had been a punishment. Tomkinson smirked.

'No sir. Canary Run is a reg'lar thing; part of the training, like. Sure, the lads don't much care for it; but, then again, as the captain says, it's no holiday camp.'

Renton pitched in.

'As I said to you, Barrett, our job here is to keep these men alive. It wouldn't be much use letting 'em have pipe and slippers, before going up the line.'

Barrett nodded an agreement. *However you justify it.* He thought.

Finally, Lyman stepped forward. Next to Tomkinson, he looked like a child. His thin face had a yellow, jaundiced hue, perhaps some underlying liver damage, Barrett wondered fleetingly. The corporal also had a rather pointed nose and, together with his wispy whiskers, reminded Barrett of a rat. The overall impression was of a very unsavoury looking man indeed. Barrett had no doubt whatsoever that he was looking at a sadist, and he quietly speculated whether he was going to be one of the first that was strung up, in the coming days.

Renton slapped his hands together as if to say: *let's get going*.

'Right. Sumner, you go with these two...' He nodded to Smithers and Tomkinson. '...you can get your feet wet with the lads on the beach.' *Another Canary Run?* Sumner did not look altogether willing, but he quickly swilled out his mug, just the same. Renton turned to Barrett, patting him on the shoulder.

'We'll observe the morning 'hate' in the Bull Ring. Corporal Lyman here has some motivational skills that would impress General Kitchener, God rest him.' Barrett smiled wanly. The 'morning hate', he had read about, was a term used to describe the routine practise of firing indiscriminately, for an hour, toward the enemy trenches – whether or not the Germans were in sight. This new usage of the word would likely take on a completely different meaning, he reckoned. After Sumner and the NCOs had left, Renton eyed Barrett over his steaming teacup.

'Sorry I couldn't join you last night, laddie. I had a little...business...to attend to, in town.' He winked slyly, but kept his eyes fixed on Barrett's. Barrett felt as if he was being tested. *Easy now.*

'Oh?' Barrett said, eyebrows raised. 'Sounds intriguing.' Barrett wasn't sure if this would turn out to be important; but, any confidence he could broker was worthwhile, as far as he was concerned. Renton smiled devilishly.

'Oh yes, indeed. Intriguing is one word you might call her.' *Ah, maybe not.* Renton went on.

'Yes, there's a lovely little bitch I've wanted to get into for some time. No joy last night, but I'm breaking in soon, let me tell you, laddie.' Renton was not describing some romantic courtship here. Clearly, it was some bordello conquest, *shared with his new pal, Barrett!* Wondering how to respond, the moment was thankfully interrupted by the entrance of Major Davenport, coming in to refresh his teacup. He and Renton stared at each other with a look that could only be described as pure hatred. A moment of silence followed while Davenport brewed up. Renton sat, saying nothing. Simply staring. The whole episode looked as though it would end with the major leaving the room, but, just as he was about to, he turned and addressed his junior.

'Haven't you somewhere to be, captain?'

Renton smiled, though there was no humour in his eyes. He pushed himself back into the chair, disrespectfully.

'No sir. But I am pretty sure there is somewhere *you* might be needed.'

The major's face immediately coloured to a deep shade of red, seemingly going darker with every passing second. Barrett noticed that the major's cup was starting to spill tea out onto the floor, as his hand began to gently shake. Expecting an explosion of wrath, the major instead turned and walked out, slamming the door behind him.

'Fucking coward.' Renton whispered, staring at the door for a lingering moment. When he turned back towards Barrett, a grin of Machiavellian glee had cracked across his face. 'The major and I don't really see eye to eye.' He winked. 'Maybe I'll tell you about it over a dram or two.' And with that, he leapt to his feet, grabbing his cap and stick. 'Come on. Let's go.'

London, April 11th, 2142

09:10 hrs

Charlotte Pilgrim, Senior Government Supervisor, signalled for Barrett to stand beside her at a large, illuminated screen desk. The desk was a newer, more sophisticated affair than Barrett was used to, but it seemed to operate in the same way. The touch screen allowed the rapid movement of files, images and so on, around the 'workspace'. In front of them was a collage of documents, most of them digital reproductions of old papers, pamphlets and photographs. Pilgrim reached across to an image showing an old man's face. Dragging it into the centre, she used the index fingers of both hands to enlarge its size. Its resolution was terribly pixelated, obliterating all definition. Clearly, the picture had been taken long before decent digital image capture. Pilgrim double-tapped the image lightly and the AI engine enhanced the face to a crisp clarity, as if it had been taken yesterday. The shot showed a man of senior years, perhaps mid-seventies, head angled slightly away from the photographer. Pilgrim began her briefing, from memory.

'This is Alistair Renton, a British national, born just outside Glasgow, 1880; died, Camberwell, 1952.' Barrett shuddered inwardly. A face from two hundred years ago. Of course, he'd seen plenty of images from this era; it wasn't that. Pilgrim went on.

'From our research into his life, he'd served as a Captain in the British Army during the first world war, Second Royal Scots. He fought at Mons, the first real engagement between the British Expeditionary Force and the Germans, in 1914.'

Barrett nodded. He was very familiar with the period, including all the major battles; but there was no way he was going to interrupt the Supervisor's flow.

'At Mons he was wounded and evacuated home. He was also awarded military honours. Sometime later -- dates are sketchy from here on -- he went back to France and, subsequently, managed to survive the war.' Barrett, gauging Pilgrim's pause, interjected.

'Well then, he was a very lucky man. I have done quite a bit of research into this history; to have gone back up the line after a 'Blighty wound' -- they used to call it – and then to survive the war, he must have had a guardian angel watching over him.'

Pilgrim turned to Barrett with a slightly frosty smile.

'Yes, Barrett; we are of course, very aware of your extra-curricular interests. You are not standing here by chance.'

Barrett inwardly scowled at the implied rebuke: *you called me into this because a computer picked my name out of a hat, you pompous bitch.*

Pilgrim, perhaps recognising her own imperiousness, readjusted to a warmer, more maternal countenance, giving some credit for Barrett's input.

'You are correct though, Barrett. What is likely to have helped his survival, we have found, is that he served, for a time, in a training camp called Étaples. The camp acted as a sort of preparatory stage for soldiers to get to peak readiness before moving up to the front.'

The name Étaples was familiar to Barrett, but he could not quite place it. Pilgrim continued.

'After the war, Renton lived out his life in England. He retired from the Army and was too old to serve in the second war. He went on to be employed in a managerial role in a textile firm until he retired. He never married, had no children; essentially a rather uneventful existence from what we could find.' Pilgrim stopped to look at Barrett, as he made the obvious inquiry.

'Since we are looking at him, I presume that something about this has changed, ma'am?' Barrett asked.

'Indeed.' Pilgrim swiped in a new screen from the left of the desk. This one showed what appeared to be a computer-generated read-out, akin to a crime scene report Barrett had often had to complete.
Name: Renton, A.
Rank: Captain
Superintendent (Discipline and Training), B-Company, Étaples Depot, France

Barrett's eyes jumped further down the screen, locking onto several lines in bold.
Likely death: **Murdered**
Time frame: **9 Sep 1917 – 15 Sep 1917**
Resolution certainty: **97%**

Barrett looked at Pilgrim with consternation. The Supervisor nodded as if in answer to the detective's unasked question. *Renton's death was the ripple.* Barrett reached across and pulled the mugshot back into view.

'I don't understand. How is it that we can we see this image of him? I mean, if he died, as it says here, in 1917, he didn't reach old age.'

Pilgrim sighed with a look that suggested she had neither the time nor inclination to go over things again.

'Remember what Henrik told you. *This* is a ripple. An episode that should not have happened. The cause and effect loop connects, like a piece of string between here...' indicating the dates on the screen, '...and our newly adjusted future - 2488. Cause...and effect. We can see Renton's photograph, read his history as if we were still on the same timeline, but that ripple...' pointing again at the bold words '...that changes our future.' She looked hard at Barrett. 'Our systems have predicted a 97% level of accuracy that he will be murdered between those dates. Our analysis has revealed a very important event occurring at that time, at that place.' Pilgrim was about to continue, when Barrett's expression changed to one of sudden realisation.

'The mutiny. Of course, that's why I remember the name; there was a revolt there, between these dates?' Pilgrim nodded, clearly impressed.

'Yes, you know your stuff, Barrett. This period of British military history, though never made secret, certainly has not been highlighted much in the history books. The days between the 9th and the 15th of September 1917, were a blight on the whole British military esprit de corps.'

Barrett, drawing back into his memory of reading about the event, could see one or two newspaper articles parked at the edge of the desk screen. Presuming the Supervisor wouldn't mind, he pulled them into the workspace and enlarged them. They mainly focussed on the aftermath of the mutiny, or on the one or two more celebrated mutineers who had evaded the army and police, for a time, after the war. These were either later apprehended and executed for treason or, in one case, chased down and shot in open countryside. Pilgrim resumed her brief.

'As you may know, rather than the messy slaughter that would have likely ensued if steps had been taken to forcefully put down the mutiny, it was left to dissipate more naturally, which it did; but not before some of the training staff had been hunted down and killed.'

Barrett turned to the Supervisor, making the connections.

'And you think Renton has become one of these casualties?' Pilgrim shrugged.

'Seems the most plausible explanation, don't you think?' She patted the side of the screen desk. 'Taking all available data and running the numbers, our systems make this the strongest conclusion, by a sizeable margin. Of course, we do not know the detail, and as they say, the devil is in the detail. Which is where you come in Detective.' She smiled at Barrett, attempting to make her earlier air of superiority a thing of the past. 'We don't know exactly when the murder will take place, nor by whom. We need, therefore, a man on the ground. Someone who can blend in, aided by an encyclopaedic knowledge of the time period, someone who can evaluate the lay of the land, as it were; someone with the proven skills of a professional detective investigator, all iced on top with the unique advantage of historical hindsight.' Pilgrim paused to draw breath.

'When you stop to consider it, we caught a break really.' She said, causing Barrett to arch an eyebrow. She continued. 'Investigating a murder during one of the costliest bloody slaughters in human history is a little ironic, don't you agree?'

She had a point. Barrett acknowledged. Pondering the supervisor's words, he also recollected that only five days following the end of the mutiny, the battle of Passchendaele had commenced, featuring some of the most appalling numbers of deaths of the war. 'Catching a break' was a fair description; had the likely timeframe extended into that period: good luck preventing a 'murder' in the midst of all that.

Northern France, September 7th, 1917

09:15 hrs

The Bull Ring screamed with activity. As Barrett approached, with Renton a pace ahead of him, he could see hundreds of soldiers marching to and fro. Entire brigades of different troops performing all manner of drill manoeuvres: compliments on the march, changing step, about turns, left wheels, right wheels, slow march, quick march, present arms, shoulder arms...it went on, endlessly. The variety of soldier was also impressive. Scots, their kilts sashaying in time with their heavy booted footfalls; Kiwis and Australians, their 'slouch' hats - brims folded up on one side, giving them an almost nonchalant, devil-may-care look; regular Tommies from practically every regiment in existence; all seemed to be here. Barrett was astounded at the sheer enormity of it. His wonder was cut short, however, by the slap of Renton's cane, suddenly creating a barrier across his chest, stopping him in his tracks. With his free hand, the captain pointed to a corner of the parade ground, a grin widening across his face.

'Over there...' he said, nodding once in that direction. '...Lyman.'

Barrett could see a large squad of men in full kit, tin helmets and rifles. From this distance he could see them all jumping on the spot; oddly though, not over an obstacle or negotiating an obstruction...just jumping, up and down, over and over, their knees, coming up towards their chests. In front, walking back and forth, holding a yard stick between his hands, was the slight form of Lyman, his slashed peak cap looking ridiculously enormous atop his stick-thin figure. As the officers neared, Barrett could see Lyman occasionally swing the yard stick outwards, with the whip-crack speed of a striking cobra, rapping knees that were not reaching the acceptable height. Unlike either Smithers or Tomkinson, Lyman was not yelling. Barrett could see his mouth moving, saying something to the men in his charge, but it was only when he got much closer that he could hear.

'Higher, you fackin' worm, you...' His cockney accent, just audible, but for all that, spiteful and vindictive. 'Call yourself a soldier? 'Ow you gonna get out of a fackin' shell 'ole if you can't do a couple a little jumps? You lazy, good-for-nothin'.'

The jumping men looked physically exhausted already, and Barrett wondered just how long they'd been performing this exercise. He glanced at his wristwatch; it was only 9.25 am. He could see the sweat pouring from their foreheads. The men wore packs on both their backs and across their chests; the pack in front, loosely hanging by attachments to their field webbing, bounced upwards with each jump, hitting the soldiers in the face. The repetition of the jumps, Barrett could see, was working some of their equipment loose; now and then, a water canteen or a mess tin would break free, tumbling onto the hard ground with a clatter. This brought a fresh tirade of abuse from Lyman, delivered in the same, low volume, obscenity-riddled invective.

Seeing the officers, Lyman temporarily broke off, running up to the captain...stamp, salute. Renton simply stared at the jumping men, hands on his hips, nodding, not registering Lyman's presence. Barrett took the opportunity.

'Field punishment, Corporal Lyman?' Barrett enquired, wondering what infringement had caused this particular penalty. Lyman's jaundiced eyes peered out from under the peak, with a slightly confused look.

'No sir.' He said, simply. Barrett could almost predict the sadist's thought: *you 'ain't seen the 'alf of it yet.* The little corporal turned his attention back to his work, instantly dropping back into his former modus operandi. Barrett glanced at Renton, gauging what he thought. As expected, the captain's face simply indicated a general look of contentment and approval. As they made to continue their 'inspection' of B-Company, Lyman's barracking seemed to increase, *probably showing off to the Boss*, Barrett imagined.

One of the soldiers was struggling more than the rest. His jumps had reduced to small hops, and Barrett could see the man's face; he looked to be on the verge of fainting. Lyman, however, was having none of it.

'Get up, you snivelling little shit.' Lyman snarled. 'I won't have you embarrassing me.' The yard stick swung again, the metal tip of the thin end, striking the soldier's backside. It would have been very painful, Barrett could see that, yet the soldier made no sound. Neither did his jumps improve. Lyman looked as if he was about to repeat the blow, when a voice was heard from somewhere further back, amongst the mass of pogoing troops.

'Why don't you leave him alone, you can see he's done.' At this, Renton stopped walking and peered into the group. Lyman's quiet venom turned suddenly into fury. Racing around the front of the pack, he screamed in a falsetto voice.

'Who said that?' The words were literally spat out of his mouth with a viciousness that took Barrett by surprise, though he quickly remembered that he had seen this behaviour before. Such a switch from relative calm to utter ferocity signified tendencies he had witnessed in more than one sociopath. No one replied, of course. They continued to jump; the culprit anonymous in the busy-ness of the 'exercise'. Barrett glanced at Renton to intervene, but Renton simply smiled, with a slight nod as if to say: *watch this.*

'Right, stop, the lot of you, stand to attention.' Lyman shouted. He seemed to have restored his emotional control just as quickly as he'd lost it.

Oh yes, Barrett thought, *you are certifiable alright.*

Lyman stood staring at the men for a long moment. Every one of the soldiers, trying hard to regain their breath, looked straight ahead, not making eye contact with their quarry.

'I give you five seconds for the one who said that to step forward, otherwise your rations will be forfeit for today, and you will all be taking the Canary Run.' His voice rose up expectantly at the end.

'One, two...' At this, a soldier stepped forward, one pace. Barrett saw the corner of Renton's mouth arch upwards slightly; a smile of satisfaction.

'March over here.' Lyman shouted.

The soldier properly right turned and marched around to the front, to stand before the corporal. He was just coming to the halt, when Lyman drove the pommel of his yard stick into the man's solar plexus. The soldier, already exhausted, doubled over instantly, coughing and retching in pain. In a smooth, fluid movement, Lyman took two steps back and again swung the stick, this time with both hands, as if taking a golf shot. The hard, brass pommel connected this time with the underside of the soldier's chin, with a sickening crunch. The soldier, who had been bent over, presenting an easy target for the blow, went sailing backwards through the air, landing hard on his backpack. Barrett felt, rather than saw, something stir in the group.

Standing.

Watching.

It was the kind of discomfort one experiences from being in the presence of a large, unpredictable dog, whose hackles have just risen up. The men were no longer looking straight ahead, but at the prone figure.

Barrett initially thought the soldier had been knocked unconscious, but the man started to make a deep-throated groaning sound. He rolled slowly off his pack, which must have been pressing hard into his back, and his mouth began spewing a steady stream of blood. The moment seemed to be playing out in slow motion. The soldier was struggling to roll into a position so he could stand, and the blood kept on pouring. Barrett slowly realised that the man had bitten through his tongue; obviously the yard stick had snapped his jaw shut, on impact. As he saw this, so too did the men, and one or two of them moved forwards, imperceptibly. Lyman, from the corner of his eye, also registered the movement.

'Stand still.' He cried, though Barrett thought he detected a faint quiver in the canary's voice. The shout checked the movement momentarily, but the tension remained, palpably ominous. Renton, perhaps sensing the sudden change in atmosphere, stepped forward, simultaneously shouting out words of command.

'Orderlies!' From the side of the parade square, two military police, their red caps clear in the cool morning sunlight, came running across. Renton addressed the squad with a calm, but stern voice.

'You men stand still. You heard the corporal. Unless you want to spend a few days on the wire...' He pointed his own stick towards the perimeter fence, where Barrett could count at least a dozen men undergoing Field Punishment Number One. The captain's threat, or perhaps just the fact that they were being spoken to by an officer, seemed to halt the simmering unrest.

For now, the men stood still.

An hour later, the two officers sat at a large picnic bench, some few hundred metres from the Bull Ring. Behind them, a large cart was parked, connected, at the far end, to a massive Clydesdale horse, its nose buried in a large feed bag that had been pulled over its head. On the back of the cart, a wide pan of cinders heated a large, cylindrical boiler, with a tap at the bottom, dispensing piping hot water into the enamel teacups of men, queueing in a long line behind. Barrett gazed at the snake of troops: judging their stances, their expressions, looking for tell-tale signs, like the one he'd detected earlier. It took him a moment to realise he himself was being watched. Renton was staring at him through a pall of cigarette smoke, exhaling the contents of his woodbine. Barrett offered him a weak smile. Renton, in return, pointed his cigarette towards him.

'You don't approve of the methods here, do you?' It wasn't an accusation. Renton was giving his fatherly smile again. Barrett paused; he hadn't realised it had been so obvious. Renton continued. 'It's fine, laddie. You can speak your mind.' He said, showing a magnanimous side that Barrett felt only surfaced amongst *chosen* confidantes. Barrett hesitated a moment longer. He sensed this offered camaraderie might be transient, especially if he gave the wrong answers. Thus far, he'd gauged Renton as cruel, ruthless and somewhat self-delusional, but he was no idiot. He decided an element of truth was, perhaps, the safest path.

'Sir, you've been doing this far longer than I...' Renton waved this off with some modesty. '...it's just that...well...you mentioned the French before...you know...their mutiny.' Barrett knew of the recent capitulation, where a huge number of French had refused to fight; there had been a mass laying down of arms that had come close to threatening the outcome of the war. Renton had referred to it when they'd first met. The captain's reaction was not what Barrett expected.

'You worry that our men would do the same?' He took in another lungful of smoke and rubbed his chin. 'It's not inconceivable,' he admitted. 'Christ knows, we've had enough deserters.' He pointed over Barrett's head, in the direction of the beach. 'We know there are bands of them, out there...in the dunes, in the town even, hiding out.' He looked back at Barrett, smiling through the smoke. 'Now and again we catch a few. But they're a minority.' He paused, leaning back on the bench. 'You keep the rotten apples out of the barrel...that's the key.' Contemplating his own words, he glanced at the men lining up for a brew. 'The vast majority of these will do what is asked of them. Have no fear of that.' He looked back at Barrett and winked. 'Besides, most know we've got the Hun on the run now. Messines Ridge put the wind up them, and from what I have heard on the grapevine, there's a fresh offensive being planned for Passchendaele, week after next.'

Messines Ridge, Barrett recalled, had been the name of a sapper-fielded operation to dig mines below the German trenches. The seeding of explosives into these mines, and their subsequent detonation, had been one of the largest blasts then encountered in wartime. Renton was right, it had been a great British success. Likewise, there was indeed a fresh offensive that would be driven forward at Passchendaele; Barrett knew how this would claim many more thousands of British and German lives...but what he also knew, that Renton didn't, at least not yet, was that the 'Hun' were far from finished, and that the war would rage on, for well over a year, before the end.

London, April 11th, 2142

12:30 hrs

Barrett closed the program down. His reading had been comprehensive but, on this occasion, in no way enjoyable. He had so often relished reading twentieth-century wartime history; all the period details, often trying to imagine himself in one theatre or another. Now he was going to *be* in one such theatre. Interest had waned considerably.

After Pilgrim's briefing, he had been escorted down to Horizon's laboratories. Through several security points, each time gazing into the blinding white light of retinal scanners, he was at last shown into a large, mostly glass walled room. Dozens of lab-coated men and women scurried around, carrying consoles filled, no doubt, with important clinical results and data. He was introduced to the senior in charge of the 'device' – Doctor Wilkins – a breezy, middle-aged woman with a shock of bright red hair and an irritatingly nasal American accent. Holding the back of Barrett's elbow, she propelled him through an adjoining door, past a wall placard that read: Strictly no unauthorised admittance. The next room was enormous. Its high ceiling gave it an audible, music hall-style echo as he walked across the highly polished floor. In front, a massive cylindrical object, around twenty metres in diameter, perhaps sixty metres long. Cables and wire looms of all colours and sizes snaked across to the cylinder, giving it a slightly unnerving, living being appearance. Wilkins motioned to a door on one end of the behemoth.

'That's the way in, but we cannot enter in our currently dirty state.' She grinned toothily. 'Of course, there is no way we can completely sterilise you; to get all those pesky microbes off you would take some pretty lethal doses of rad...and then there'd be no point sending you.' She said in a folksy, shucks-type mannerism that did nothing to ease Barrett's apprehension. She went on to explain the operation of the 'device', something about how a human's physical pattern could be disassembled, down to a sub-atomic level, necessary to be transported along the very same time string that joined the ripple event of the past, to the disturbingly vacant future.

Barrett had politely nodded during this 'lecture', not understanding a single word of it. There had also been some talk of the 'astronomical' amount of energy required for the transfer. Zoning out of the technobabble he had, instead, focussed on Wilkins' annoying voice, especially the amount of times she called him 'bucko'. He remembered her jubilantly applauding herself and her team – but mainly herself – on how the testing phases of transferring matter across time had been extremely successful. There was a suggestion that this had not always been so, but he had asked no further questions on *that* subject. Wilkins was a little too confident in her ability to place Barrett in an exact time and location of her choosing, for his liking. In his experience, such hubris usually preceded a monumental failure. What was the old saying? *Pride cometh before the fuck up*...something like that anyway.

After a not very appetising meal, taken alone in quarters set aside for him, Barrett familiarised himself with the material that would cross over with him. The level of detail was admittedly impressive. The uniform of a first lieutenant from the Royal Artillery had been chosen as his cover. His infiltration was camouflaged by the likely high frequency of comings and goings, to and from the front, and he was to join Renton's staff, conveniently arranged via an authentic looking drafting document, giving him reason for being there. Of course, his arrival would come as a complete surprise; no-one would have been informed, but then again, *c'est la guerre.* He pulled on the infuriatingly itchy jacket. It reminded him of the ancient hair shirts that he had read monks used to wear, as a mental challenge of their faith. How could anyone fight a war in such discomfort, he wondered. The fit of the jacket was, predictably, perfect to his dimensions. He knew the trousers and boots would be the same, but dressed into them, nevertheless, standing before the full-length mirror, looking himself up and down. Would he pass for a British Army officer? He saluted himself, feeling somewhat oafish, despite being alone. Other than his clothes, his only other possessions included a knapsack, a wind-up wristwatch, a brown leather wallet containing some huge, historically accurate paper money -- fifteen pounds -- and his I.D. card. He was a little disappointed that no weapon had been provided. He would have to source one, once there, an obstacle that should not present a problem for a commissioned officer. He had read various texts that indicated that respect for the officer cadre was, generally, a 'God-given' right. Other than during the rare exception of a full, widespread, murderous mutiny, of course, he mused dolefully.

After a fitful night's sleep, Barrett, once again, back in the laboratory, was administered a range of tablets by the cheerful Wilkins. They had to be taken every day for the week building up to zero hour. He could expect some 'odd' effects, as they did their 'magic', she nonchalantly informed him - but only after he had swallowed the first batch of pills, he noted. Some dizziness? Perhaps. Some bizarre cravings for food? Maybe. Some quick 'pit stops to the john'? Definitely. It was a cocktail of drugs designed to prepare his system for the 'rigours of the voyage'. Certainly, they would help him to cope better with the expected nausea, following infiltration. Wilkins further explained that he would be disoriented 'on arrival', but the effects would be short-lived. Barrett's rolled eyes drew a flash of ire from the scientist.

'A small price to pay for redefining the laws of physics, bucko.' She said petulantly.

Barrett apologised, but resented the burn from the lab rat.

You're not the one getting his molecules scrambled to save the world's collective backsides, darling.

Barrett worked hard to restore Wilkins' bruised ego, and, after some interested nods and facial expressions of appreciation, Barrett asked the important question.

'What's the drill for exfil?'

Nothing much had been discussed around the subject of exfiltration. It had been explained that the return transfer back would initiate following a finite time period. Transit would automatically commence several days following the expiry of the timeframe, within which Renton was predicted to be murdered. As imprecise as this seemed, it was simply a matter of practicality, he was told. Obviously, he could not be pulled back before the 'job' was done, before the subject was safely through the critical time window. Neither could he exactly radio for a pickup. The process just had to follow a sequence. Whilst Barrett was as content as he could be -- as far as getting *in* was concerned -- the getting *out* part troubled him. Wilkins nodded sympathetically.

'OK, let me try to explain it.' She clearly did not relish trying to dumb-down a lifetime of theoretical knowledge and wisdom for the benefit of this flat-foot cop. 'Of course, no transfer chamber exists in the past, right? However, what you must appreciate is that your existence in that period is alien. *You shouldn't be there, bucko.* In fact, from the very moment you arrive, Mother Nature is trying to expel you.' Barrett raised an eyebrow at that; Wilkins acknowledged it. 'Look, all I am trying to say is that your physical chemistry is at odds with the environment; it has, for want of a better expression, a shelf-life. Once past a certain threshold, one we have been able to adjust and predict, your molecular cohesion will, once more, disassemble...'

Barrett's face showed alarm. Wilkins patted his arm reassuringly.

'...relax, you're not gonna start melting, like the Wicked Witch of the East.' Wilkins chuckled, genuinely amused by her reference. 'No, this process will be instantaneous...like that!' She snapped her fingers. 'In just the same method as you go out, in fact. It is only once you have been...dematerialised, shall we say...only then will we be able to pull you back, through the same connected time loop as before.'

Barrett nodded, more in acceptance than understanding; but then a thought struck him.

'What if this happens whilst I am stood in front of someone?'

Wilkins shrugged her shoulders and spread her hands out in a gesture of *whatever.*

-15-

Northern France, September 7th, 1917

21:30 hrs

Feeling every rut and pothole in the road, Barrett glanced sideways at Lieutenant Sumner. The young man's left thigh pressed into Barrett's right. On the other side, another captain, who Renton had briefly called 'Bert', completed the sardined arrangement on the rear bench seat of the car. Renton was in front, next to the driver – the adjutant, Simmons. Barrett couldn't move much, but he'd been assured, *'...it wasn't far, to Shangri La'.* Sumner didn't look too bad, *physically,* considering he'd had the pleasure of the Canary Run to Étaples beach, for most of his day. However, Barrett's sideways glance told him that the second lieutenant was not happy. His face certainly exhibited signs of stress: thin white lips, creased forehead, and he'd barely said two words, whilst waiting for the pick-up. Renton had organised this little field trip, to 'let everyone's hair down', as he had put it. Something about 'experiencing the pleasures of France' had revealed the captain's intentions to Barrett, who had inwardly sighed once he'd put two and two together. He hadn't envisaged a bordello visit as part of his mission, and that was a fact. As the car rumbled across the bridge, over the River Canche, separating the camp from the town, Barrett contemplated again the growing tension he had witnessed in the Bull Ring earlier. He knew that this was merely the tip of the iceberg, that incidents like that one were starting to happen everywhere around the camp. The fuse had been lit and, in only two days' time, there would come an explosion.

The car pulled into the main street cutting through Étaples town. Past several cafes and estaminets, Barrett could see officers -- and it was *just* officers, at the moment -- sitting out front, smoking cigarettes and cigars, drinking wine, entertaining young ladies, and each other, completely oblivious to the rising storm. The car harshly braked to a halt and both captains eagerly exited, leaving the two lieutenants to uncoil themselves. Sumner turned briefly to Barrett, a pained expression across his face.

'Is this a mandatory requirement, sir?' He asked sheepishly. Barrett, who was far from thrilled himself, smiled at the young man with some empathy.

'No one can make you do anything you don't want to, Lionel.' He patted the lieutenant's knee as he extricated himself from the car. '...and, it's Liam, remember.' He glanced down at Sumner's left hand. No wedding band. He contemplated the man's reticence. *He must have a sweetheart back home*, he thought, and then briefly: *A virgin? Unlikely, but not out of the question in this era.*

The two men stood, looking up at the building before them. The gaudily painted sign above the door left nothing to the imagination. *Le Jardin d'Eden.* A few steps led up to the front door, where Renton stood waving them to join him, his eyes glinted in the light from the streetlamps, as if they were on fire; Barrett could have sworn he saw the man lick his lips, like some hungry wolf.

Inside the lobby, a short woman with jet black hair approached the men. Around her shoulders, a sheer, almost transparent garment hung down the rounded curves of her hips; Barrett could make out her plump white thighs through the material. As she came close, Renton greeted her with jocular familiarity.

'Ah, Dominique.' He kissed her offered hand. Still holding it, he turned her around to his companions, by way of introduction. 'Men, may I present the reason for fighting in this God-forsaken country...Madame Dominique, the owner of the Garden...' he looked back at the Madame, leeringly. '...and one hell of a woman.'

Madame Dominique smiled thinly; it was clear she'd heard it all before. She looked at 'Bert', giving him a polite nod; not the first visit for the captain, it seemed. Turning her attention to the two lieutenants, she looked them up and down, seeming to take in their forms with an expert eye. Sidling up to Barrett, she reached up and caressed his cheek.

'You have a kind face, Monsieur...' Her heavy make-up tried desperately to conceal her age; Barrett estimated her fortieth birthday had passed by some time ago. '...but...' she paused, gazing deeply, as if into Barrett's soul. '...you have very sad eyes.'

Renton brayed laughter, but this did not disturb the Madame; she continued to look on, seemingly oblivious to the captain's mirth, behind her. Barrett smiled back. A woman of her experience would have seen a great deal, he thought; *but you have no idea, sister.*

Turning to Sumner, she stopped, as if through some sudden shock of electricity. Staring into his face, her own broke into a warm smile. She stroked his shoulder kindly.

'Ah Monsieur, I...'

Sumner interrupted her suddenly, and somewhat stiffly, speaking in rapid, fluent French. Barrett and the two captains looked at each other, mouths agape. None of them knew what Sumner said, but whatever it was, it made the Madame giggle slightly and effect a short shrug of her shoulders.

'Tres bien.' She said and turned back to Renton.

With a click of her fingers, several women appeared from multiple doorways and alcoves in the brightly lit lobby. Barrett was about to ask Sumner what he'd said, but before he could, a girl stood before him, blocking out all other things. *Shit, this is happening too fast.* He thought, feeling suddenly very young and naive. The girl reached out and took hold of his hand, pulling his arm up to tow him along. Her hand was warm and unbelievably soft.

He followed.

Inside the girl's bedroom, the lighting was subdued by bolts of thin, transparent cloth draped over the light shades, creating a sensual, if somewhat gloomy, environment. The room was very warm, and a fug of heavy perfume filled the air, making Barrett want to cough and clear his throat. The girl, who had been pulling Barrett along by the hand, stopped and turned to face him. Her long brown hair swung in an arc around her as she turned, revealing a long slender neck. Her skin was porcelain white, though she did not look anaemic. He reckoned she was no more than twenty years old, which made him feel both sad, and not a little libidinous. If his estimates were correct, she may well have started her 'trade' at the beginning of the war – that being so, at maybe aged sixteen or seventeen, tops. His own age of thirty-seven notwithstanding, he also imagined, in that moment, a daughter that he and Monica might have had, in another life. He sighed and sat down in the empty chair at the foot of the girl's bed. The girl kneeled down before him, trying to place her palms on his knees. Barrett's hands overlaid hers, holding them firmly, resisting the gentle pressure she applied to splay his knees apart.

'No.' He said simply, with a short shake of his head. The girl looked up into his eyes, a look that seemed to indicate growing confusion. She spoke. Very good English, if deeply accented.

'I...I don't understand.' She said, softly. 'Do I...am I not...' She searched for the words; Barrett tried to console.

'Forgive me; you are very attractive, but...let's...can we just talk for a while?' The girl continued to look uncertain, but eventually nodded, slowly. Her eyes continued to search his, trying to fathom this strange soldier. Barrett smiled.

'What's your name?' he asked, returning the look into her deep brown eyes. The girl slowly climbed to her feet, somewhat awkwardly, teetering on her high heeled, strappy shoes. Barrett momentarily pictured a new-born foal trying to stand for the first time. The girl, successfully upright, perched herself carefully on the edge of the bed.

'I am called Simone.' She said quietly, looking down at her feet. Then, as if a thought came to her: 'Is there something you want, I should do?' She enquired, eager to please. Barrett continued to smile, reassuringly. Again, he shook his head.

'No...really...just talk. Is that OK? Just to talk.' The girl shrugged an acceptance, stood once more and walked over to a sideboard, where two glasses and a demijohn sat on a silver-plated platter. She lifted the demijohn, looking enquiringly at Barrett. He nodded acquiescence; *a taste of wine would be good right about now*, he thought. She splashed the red into both glasses and brought them over. As Barrett took the glass, she lightly touched the base of hers against the side of his. *Cheers.* Sitting back down, she stared into his eyes, touching the wine to her lips.

'I have met plenty of British soldiers...but only one other like you, Monsieur.' With one foot, she toed the strap off the heel of her other foot, letting the shoe hang loosely, playfully looped over her toes. 'Most men want to get straight to it...no talking'. Barrett said nothing. He imagined that was the general way of things. She went on. 'This other man, he also liked to talk. He had a wife...' She trailed off, as if this was explanation enough. She eyed him across the rim of her glass. 'Do you have a wife?'

No. Not for a long, long time.

'Yes,' he said. 'She is waiting for me...in England,' he lied. He was ready for the next inevitable question.

'So why you come here...if you have a wife?' She took a sip, then went on to answer her own question. 'Lots of men have wives...it does not stop them.' Barrett took a large mouthful of wine; it was surprisingly good. He looked into the dark red liquid; she'd made a good point. He smiled back at the girl.

'I have a wife, and I am faithful to her...' He sat back comfortably in the chair. '...but...I still love women.' He motioned his glass around the room. 'To speak with women, to...smell women...' he looked back to Simone meaningfully. 'To *see* women...I am still a human being, *mon cherie.*'

She laughed suddenly, no doubt in response to his somewhat pathetic application of the language. *Not like old Sumner...the sly dog.* She swung her legs up onto the bed, leaning on one elbow as she surveyed the lieutenant. She was relaxing, Barrett thought - perhaps knowing that she did not have to perform, for once.

'So, you just come here to...look.' More a statement that a question.

'And to talk...' Barrett reminded her, enjoying how the conversation was becoming playful.

'And to talk.' She agreed, before saying: 'So...if we are to...just talk, I must know your name, no?'

Barrett laughed. *Another reasonable point.*

'My name is Liam.' He said, dispensing with the surname.

'So, how long are you here?' She nodded towards the wall, as if seeing through to the adjoining rooms. 'Your colleagues have been visiting us a lot.'

Barrett nodded. This he knew well. His Mess acquaintances -- his fellow lieutenants -- had revealed that the camp commandant, Brigadier General Thomas, had taken great pains to establish a clinic in the camp hospital – purely to cope with the unprecedented increase in venereal diseases amongst the commissioned staff. He wondered whether to tell her that his stay wouldn't be long, but immediately decided not to – *keep things simple.* Instead, he returned to her previous comment.

'Do they treat you well enough?' He asked. Simone pondered that for a moment.

'Most of the time, oui. Dominique has very strict rules, but some...' a slight shrug, '...they get carried away. We understand. It has been a long war, monsieur. Many who have passed through here are probably gone now.' Her gaze drifted momentarily, and Barrett wondered briefly is she'd ever allowed herself to get close to one of her clients. Noticing Barrett's glass was empty, she eased herself off the bed, moving to pour him a refill.

Just then, a sudden, loud shattering noise of breaking glass cut through the tranquil peace. This was immediately followed by a scream and several shouts. Barrett leapt to his feet, making it to the door just ahead of Simone. In the corridor, several doors had opened to emit partially clad occupants, peering out, looking to see what the commotion was. Barrett saw the fleeting glimpse of a naked girl running away down the corridor; her cries were shrill, and he thought he discerned the word: 'violer'...*what was that?*

Out from the same doorway, Renton stepped; his vest, the only garment still worn. He glanced after the fleeing woman, then turned to see Barrett staring at him. Barrett could see a pencil-thin line of blood across the captain's left cheek. Renton's eyes fixed Barrett's for only a second. That was all it took. It was a look Barrett had seen on numerous occasions. He turned back to Simone.

'I think we may have to leave now...' he said apologetically. 'May I see you again?' Simone arched an eyebrow.

'To talk?' She asked and, despite the furore down the corridor, cracked a warm smile. Barrett smiled back.

Around ten minutes later, Barrett stood in the lobby, listening to the ongoing argument between Renton and Madame Dominique. He could have quite happily left them to it; it was very clear what had occurred. As Simone had said, some of the men 'get carried away' – Renton's companion obviously thought so. The stare Renton had given him in the upper corridor, however, troubled him. The whole episode suggested more than sex play, taken too far. He had seen venom in that stare; he had seen *murder*. Several prostitutes walked past him, each giving an, understandably, unwelcome look. Captain 'Bert' was nowhere to be seen; however, walking casually down the stairwell, came Sumner, looking much more confidant and at ease than he had done earlier. He looked at Barrett enquiringly.

'What's going on?' he asked, nodding to the passageway from where all the din was coming from. Barrett sighed, rubbing his forehead with the palm of one hand.

'It appears our leader has outstayed his welcome.' He looked at Sumner. 'You seem better. And you certainly have a good handle on the lingo'. Referring to the young man's earlier conversation with the Madame.

'Yes, I'm fine. It wasn't as bad as I'd imagined. Nerves, I guess. And yes, it does help to have a few words. My family would holiday out here most years.' Sumner replied.

Barrett nodded. He'd never needed to learn another language; his console's translate function made it all so easy. A thought occurred to him.

'Lionel, what does 'violer' mean?' Sumner furrowed his brow slightly before answering.

'Well, it does depend a little on the context; but, commonly, it means *rape.*'

London, April 16th, 2142

09:45 hrs

Barrett sat quietly, meditating for a little while longer before he was called down. He wore a thin, sterile paper suit, so flimsy, he thought, that it would tear open with the smallest of movements. He glanced over to the tray beside him; the remnants of a meal lay, cold, picked through. The week's daily diet of meds had weaned him off food for the most part and now he felt like his stomach was full of nothing but gas, making him feel bloated and uncomfortable. He picked up the hand console, for perhaps the hundredth time, to look over the mission details. It included maps of the nearby town of Étaples; cafes and estaminets; the two town brothels: Le Jardin d'Eden and 290; one or two faces that may be important, one of them being a Major Davenport, B-Company's CO, Renton's immediate superior. Unlike the image of old-man Renton, Davenport's showed him as a younger man; it was very grainy – not much the A.I. could do with that, Barrett supposed.

Anders and Pilgrim had paid him a visit the day before, all handshakes and pats on the shoulder. Their premature send-off was, like the whole week had been, part of the schedule of 'processes', *part of the plan*. To have come any later, so close to transfer, would have risked introducing bacterial microbes that would have pushed the start line backwards. They had both taken it in turns to emphasise the importance of the mission, how humankind hung on Barrett's actions, *yadda yadda*. Though trying his best to mask his internal thoughts, some slip of body language, or perhaps some minute facial tic, must have crept out, for Pilgrim, quickly, obviously, changed tack and began to wax lyrical about hero parades, promotions, financial rewards and other such nonsense.

Yeah, right. Barrett thought. *Do you seriously think this thing is going to work?*

He'd had reservations from day one, when Anders had run through his initial 'sales pitch'. He had seen plenty of material throughout the week to suggest that the plan *could* work, had seen reams of evidence showing endless trials, experiments, proof that success had the highest of probabilities; yet, the notion of sending him two hundred and twenty-five years back through time, never mind bringing him home again, was just too fantastic for him to fully accept. It didn't matter though. In the final analysis, someone had to do it, and why not him? The thought reminded him of his very last task. Touching an icon on the console, the screen changed to a digital document, the title in bold, ornamental font:

The last will and testament of...

He'd put this off until the last minute for the simple reason that it depressed him. As a Detective Investigator he had, of course, already created one - signed and locked away in the Department files. This one would be no different. After Monica had passed, he had literally no family to speak of: no children; parents long dead. Even if he'd had any significant others, there was precious little to bequeath, other than a modest, death-in-service pension. Even his vehicle was a company car. Barrett, not for the first time, pondered whether these factors had been part of the computer's selection of him, as the perfect fit. What was it that Pilgrim had said about Renton?

...a rather uneventful existence.

Well, that wasn't true *now*, was it? Renton was perhaps *the* most eventful person to have ever existed, as far as future humanity was concerned, at any rate. And, by association, this mystery man, Renton, had made Barrett almost as important.

The quiet, calm-sounding ping of an incoming voice message broke his contemplation. It was followed by Wilkins' nasal drawl informing him to prepare himself for escort, down to the lab. He knew the drill: once in the lab he'd have the opportunity for one last 'evacuation', then into his uniform and, finally, into the cylinder – the only thing he had not done before. He had a brief thought:

Please Lord, don't let Wilkins' voice be the last one I hear.

He glanced back down at his console, sighed loudly and pressed the execute button. The electronic document folded up into a facsimile of a sealed envelope and, with a *whoosh* sound, rushed off the screen. Laying the console on the small side table, he stood and waited for his chaperones.

Inside the cylinder, he lay quite still. There was little light in the chamber, but he could make out the walls, covered in what looked like bathroom tiles. He had seen similar objects, albeit much larger, plastered over the exterior of the Moon shuttles, and, more recently, the terra-forming ships, constantly leaving for Mars. Some kind of heat shield? Snaking along the walls, rows of tubing, all dotted with holes along their length, jetted a blue-white gas, reminiscent of steam, into the cylinder. The bench he lay on was of highly polished stainless steel, or aluminium – whatever it was, it was no chaise longue. Just before entering, he had changed into his army officer's uniform, all itchy and coarse. At that very moment, he thought that maybe, just maybe, this was the most uncomfortable he'd ever been in his life. A voice came to him, through the foggy interior.

'OK, bucko. We are just gonna be a few minutes here, doing our last round of checks. You just hang tight and I'll get back to you.'

Despite the annoying drawl, Barrett found Wilkins' voice surprisingly reassuring. He had started to get a little jittery as he had dressed, a feeling that had only increased as he climbed in through the cylinder door. The gloom of the interior did have a certain crypt-like quality, he determined. He expected it would have been worse, were it not for the latest little blue pills he had been administered an hour or so ago. He had stopped asking about the constant supply of drugs they'd been feeding him, but he reckoned these must have been some kind of muscle relaxant.

Trying to adjust his head into a slightly more agreeable position, he was conscious of a low hum beginning to emanate from deeper within the cylinder, down past his boots. He lifted his head off the bench, looking down the length of his body, from where this new sound came from, but he could see nothing. Its tone was increasing in intensity, however, and he could feel, more than hear, things around him beginning to vibrate. The vapour, pouring in through the wall tubes, was also increasing in pressure, making an audible hiss that tried to compete with the rising hum. Louder and louder, the hum continued to rise, starting to reach a slightly uncomfortable volume.

Was this it? Barrett felt his anxiety rising.

Wilkins hasn't come back to me yet...she said she'd come back to me!

Barrett realized he was starting to feel a mild panic. Despite his earlier reservations, he now wanted to hear the scientist's voice. He *needed* to hear it.

Just tell me it's happening, then I'll be fine.

Barrett strained to listen for Wilkins' voice. The sound was no longer a hum; no-one could have called it that anymore; now it was an ear-splitting cacophony, and he realised that no more soothing words would be audible now, even if she *were* speaking. He had the vague sensation of a rising temperature and the fleeting thought that he had to squint his eyes...*why did he need to do that?*

Then, nothing.

Northern France, September 8th, 1917

09:20 hrs

The morning following the brothel debacle found Barrett, Sumner and Renton called into Major Davenport's office. Simmons, the adjutant, had apprehended them as they walked in through the staff building entrance, from breakfast. Simmons looked worried. Barrett noticed that Renton's mood appeared to be perturbed too, though he wasn't sure why. True, the night before had been a shambles, but Renton hadn't shown much upset as they'd been driven back to camp, even with the nasty-looking cut below his left eye. Neither of the two lieutenants had asked him what had happened. Sumner's translation of what Renton's prostitute companion had said suggested that the captain's appetites had turned violent, and this was further supported by the fact that Madame Dominique had practically thrown them all out. This turn of events both pleased and depressed Barrett. In one sense, it was perhaps fortunate that they were no longer welcome at Le Jardin: *too complicated.* Yet, at the same time, Barrett had started to enjoy Simone's company. Granted, he was old enough to be her father, but he was still human.

They filed into the major's office, finding Davenport standing, looking out of his window. He motioned for them to sit around the large conference table, but he remained on his feet.

'The colonel has been to see me this morning.' He began, a stern look of reproach on his face. Barrett glanced quickly at the other two. Their expressions could not have been more different. Sumner – respectful alertness; Renton – disinterested apathy. The major continued. 'He informed me that there have been several incidents across the camp that are leading the brigadier to a rather unpleasant conclusion, in respect of your methods.'

Barrett noted that Davenport did not say *our* methods. The major nodded to Barrett and Sumner.

'You two are largely excused from this accusation, since you have only just arrived...' Renton let out a snort, knowing what was coming. '...but you, captain...your actions *are* within scope.' Renton's dark expression changed slightly; a tiny smile starting to form. He looked up at the major, sighed and replied.

'And yet, despite me being the only one culpable, you thought it necessary to bring these two in, so you could dress me down publicly?' Renton said, with an arched eyebrow. Davenport carried on as if Renton had not spoken.

'Of course, it isn't just B-Company under scrutiny. But, as far as I'm concerned, I don't care what others are doing...' As Davenport continued to speak, Renton slowly stood and walked to the door, opening it as if to leave. Davenport exploded. 'Where the bloody hell do you think you're going?' The major's face rapidly reddening with rage. Renton held the door wide and addressed the major with infuriating calmness.

'I'm going nowhere, sir...' He looked at the two lieutenants. 'They are.' He spoke quietly to Barrett and Sumner. 'Gentlemen...the grown-ups need to talk.' Barrett glanced back towards the senior officer to gauge agreement. Seeing this, Renton's voice, slightly louder, cut across the room with a menacing imperative that brooked no argument: 'Now.'

Slowly, Barrett rose out of his chair, Sumner following suit. Both men walked out and Renton closed the door softly behind them.

'What are you doing?' Sumner whispered. The two men had walked through to the lobby together, but Barrett had turned back, holding a finger to his lips to signify the need for hush. Barrett glanced back at the second lieutenant.

'Make sure Simmons doesn't come through here.' Sumner began to protest, but Barrett cut him short, putting on an accentuated mien. 'That's an order, old boy.' Tiptoeing back to the major's door, he soon recognised that his attempted stealth was superfluous. The senior officer was in full flood now, shouting at the top of his lungs.

'...that I'm your commanding officer! Never, in all my years, have I encountered anything like it. Your behaviour is insubordinate beyond belief; you question my every decision. I won't have it, I tell you.'

Barrett opened his own office door on his way past; he'd need a rapid escape route if either Renton or the major, came juggernauting out. Davenport's remonstrance went on for what seemed like an eternity, with Renton remaining silent. Eventually, the major stopped, perhaps more to draw breath than for any other reason. Renton's voice, when it came, was far quieter, more controlled, measured, *retaining the high ground* Barrett thought.

'If you are quite finished, I suggest you listen carefully now.' He said, forebodingly. 'You, my cowardly little friend, are done.' Barrett strained but could not hear anything from the major. This short sentence from Renton had obviously been enough to render the man speechless. 'I've put up with you for long enough, but my tolerance has come to an end. All you needed to do was carry on playing your part quietly, in the background, and I would have left you alone...'

Barrett heard the scrape of a chair being dragged across the wooden floor, probably Renton taking a seat for this...*whatever this was.*

'Until today, I have turned a blind eye to you skulking back here, a permanent fixture behind the lines. You've never jeopardised your sorry arse throughout this whole bloody war – you make me sick to my stomach. Yet I've never judged you...openly.' Barrett could only imagine Davenport's face. The major remained deathly quiet.

'I've run this piss-poor Company the whole time, sorting things out, doing all the shit that you deemed beneath you...YOU!' This last word came as a shout that made Barrett jump. *The sociopathic anger broaching the surface?* Barrett wondered.

'And now, just because a few of those belly aching bastards out there have complained about a bit of discipline, and you have had a wee rap on the knuckles...you find your spine enough to give me a row?' Renton chuckled in disbelief. 'You sorry, worthless prick.' It went quiet for a moment, and Barrett wondered if he needed to move. Then, quietly. 'Your time is up. I'll be making that phone call.'

At last, Davenport's voice returned, anger still detectable, but at a much-reduced volume.

'Oh yes, the phone call. You've threatened me with this before. Do what you think you must, of course, though I am no longer convinced about your 'friends in high places' routine any more...' Another pause; Barrett started to edge backwards towards his office. Davenport wasn't finished yet, though.

'Perhaps it's time *I* made a phone call too. You see, I know what you've been up to, Renton.' It was Renton's turn to go silent. Barrett imagined he detected a smile in Davenport's voice.

'Oh yes, two can play games. I know all about your chum. Now what was his name? Oh yes, Private, or should I say former Private, Jones, and his little band of bootleggers.' His voice had taken on a new confidence; he was definitely savouring Renton's discomfort. He went on. 'And I know you're up to your neck in it as well. You say I make you sick? The old soldier eh? A war hero of Mons...decorated for bravery? Oh yes, I'm well aware of how you see me, and how you see yourself.' He paused to let that sink in. 'You call me a coward? Fine, I may be; I'm not going to argue that...but you've some nerve coming all high and mighty with what you're doing...'

Barrett heard the scrape of the chair once more, Renton getting to his feet.

'...profiteering from black marketed medical supplies while good men...'

Davenport's voice abruptly ceased, replaced by the unmistakable sound of a man being winded, followed by the dull thud of a body falling to the floor. Davenport's body.

Barrett's mind raced. He felt like he should barge in, intervene, but, he couldn't. Even if Renton's sudden removal from history was the result of facing a firing squad, it was too late to change things now. Barrett's mission remained the same: he needed to keep the man alive, even if he had turned out to be a self-promoting, war-profiteering sociopath. He turned and made for his office door, certain that Renton was likely to be heading out at any moment. Just before he closed his own door, he heard Renton's last words.

133

'You can take your chances up the Line, Davenport, I'll be seeing to that. But if you utter one more word about Private fucking Jones, or my connection with him, you won't even make it that far.'

The major's door opened, as Barrett's silently closed.

-18-

Northern France, September 8th, 1917

10:30 hrs

Simmons' head popped around the edge of Barrett's door.

'Sir, sorry to disturb you, the captain wants to see you and Lieutenant Sumner in his office right away.' Barrett barely had time to lift his head to look at the adjutant; he had already gone.

Around an hour had passed since the meeting with the major. Barrett had seen neither him nor Renton since. This had given him time to ponder what he had heard, try to figure out what it all meant. From his first encounter of the two men together, it had been obvious there was bad blood. And now he knew why. Renton had been holding Davenport to ransom through the application of some unseen leverage; perhaps making use of some 'old boys' network': *you scratch my back...*

It was plausible how a geriatric like Davenport had been able to wangle a 'base wallah' job, but he had not considered, until now, how a fit, decorated officer like Renton was able to stay safely distant from the action. After all, right at this very moment, Barrett knew -- from recorded history, at any rate -- that the vast influx of troops coming from Britain were draftees, that or young volunteers without the first clue about soldiering. Renton was an army regular; his experience would have been invaluable. Yet here he was. Oh yes, he had connections alright. And, from the look of things, enough clout to unseat a major, from a cushy staff post. But what was this other mystery? The bootlegging?

Up until now, Barrett had confined the probability of Renton's murder to be the likely actions of the would-be mutineers, but as he knew, the widespread upset wasn't due to begin until tomorrow – the 9th of September. This assumed that history hadn't been altered, of course, confirming Anders' umbrella theory. Another possibility had emerged the night before, which Barrett had not been prepared for. The fracas in Le Jardin had the makings of a crime of passion. A sex game gone awry, followed by the self-defensive lash-out of a prostitute, was not out of the question. Fortunately, it seemed that Renton, indeed the entire group, were now banned from the bordello. This morning's discovery had brought a much more likely suspect to the surface, however. Davenport had more than enough motive, and that was even before Renton had dropped him, Barrett mused. And now the bootlegging angle. Smuggling military supplies during wartime was...*is*...a cardinal crime. It would not be unreasonable to assume that such skullduggery could lead to an outcome of murder. Was this to be the route to Renton's untimely demise?

Barrett entered Renton's office to find Sumner already seated. For a brief moment, Barrett contemplated whether Sumner had informed on him, about the eavesdropping. Certainly, the young lieutenant looked a bit shifty, he thought. He sat down, as Renton eyed him, scratching a match across the table to light his cigarette. He inhaled a deep lungful of smoke, looking at the two men opposite.

'Right. From our earlier meeting, it is apparent that we need to tighten things up a little round here.' His voice did nothing to betray the real outcome of his, and Davenport's, 'chat'. It was business-like, empty of emotion. 'Each of us has assignments today.' He turned to Sumner, and Barrett thought he detected something of a sneer in the captain's voice, as he addressed the young man. 'Sumner, I have a *special* duty for you, this afternoon.' He looked down at a sheet of paper. 'I have here a list of names. They are deserters that require processing.' He held Sumner's eyes fleetingly, but in that brief moment, Barrett saw something. It lasted but a millisecond; had he not been looking directly at him, he would have missed it. But it was there. The same dead-eyed expression he had seen in the corridor of Le Jardin, as the prostitute had fled from Renton's clutches. The captain smiled thinly, but there was no warmth in his eyes. 'Corporal Lyman has been briefed to assist you; he has done this several times, so just follow his lead.'

Sumner looked confused. He glanced across at Barrett, then back to Renton.

'What exactly does the duty involve, sir?' Sumner asked. Renton's painted-on smile vanished.

137

'As I said, Lyman has the details.' Sumner seemed ready to protest but was abruptly cut short. 'Dismissed, Lieutenant.' Renton barked. The harsh stare was back in place, piercing through the pall of smoke hanging in front of Renton's face.

Sumner rose to his feet, reached forward to pick up the list, and made his way out. Barrett wondered briefly if the encounter with Davenport had rattled the captain more than he first thought. This consideration was soon discounted, however, for as soon as Sumner had closed the door, Renton's expression changed yet again, this time looking at Barrett with − what seemed to be − genuine bonhomie.

'Now, Liam.'

Even stranger, Barrett thought; first name terms?

'You too have a special task.' He smiled warmly, handing over another sheet of paper. 'Yours *also* involves deserters, I'm afraid; however, these blackguards are not yet in *our* custody.' He passed another sheet of paper across the desk. 'The names on *this* list are men currently being held up the Line. Three of them were caught trying to backtrack through a supply trench; another two had given each other, what they hoped would be, Blighty wounds. They both tried to shoot each other in the foot, though I'm told one of them has ended up losing three of his toes' he said, holding in a chuckle. 'Anyway, they are all being held by one of the provost sergeants, up at Waterloo Junction.' He nodded towards the door. 'Corporals Tomkinson and Smithers have enlisted two redcaps each and are waiting for you at the armoury.' Barrett looked at the paper, but his thoughts were elsewhere. Cheerfully, nonchalantly, he asked.

'And you sir, what does the day hold for you?'

Renton did not answer immediately. Instead he stared at Barrett. He took another long drag of his cigarette, holding the inhalation for a long moment, before leaning forward, to stub it out in a clamshell ashtray.

'What do you mean?' he asked, at last. Barrett smiled disarmingly.

'You said that we *all* had assignments today. I just wondered what yours was.'

Renton's face, once more, broke into a smile.

'Oh, yes. Well, mine also involves deserters, laddie. The only difference is mine haven't been caught yet.' He stood and came around the desk, standing next to a large wall map showing the camp and surrounding areas. He pointed to the section between the camp and the sea. 'We know that many of them have been spotted in and around the sand dunes, here.' He glanced back at Barrett. 'The belief is that there are a few caves located in this area, where some of them have been hiding out.'

Bootleggers?

Internally, Barrett cursed the arrangement. He suspected Renton was telling the truth, but not the whole truth. It was clear that Barrett had caught the captain on the hop - he'd already forgotten his own story about *everyone* being issued with separate assignments – but, like the best lies -- Barrett knew well -- surrounding them with a little truth lent them credibility, especially if the lie had to be revealed later on. It seemed clear that Renton would indeed be heading for the sand dunes, but not on any hunt. Obviously, Renton had 'business' to attend to, business that, up until recently, he'd been able to conduct without two junior officers under his feet.

Was that why B-Company had been running light for so long?

In any case, Barrett could not afford to be sent on some babysitting task while Renton could potentially be in mortal danger, should his 'business' go south. He offered a suggestion, deep down knowing that Renton would not go for it.

'Sir, from what you're saying, isn't it possible that these hideaways will resist...with force? I mean...well, I mean, why don't I accompany you? I can always go and collect these others from Waterloo Junction later; it's not like they are going anywhere is it?' Renton quickly shook his head; Barrett knew it was hopeless, but he had to try.

'No laddie. Look, I appreciate your thinking, but I'll have a few redcaps of my own...' he paused, a sneering smile forming across his lips. '...besides, a few lily-livered cowards don't give me cause for concern.' Barrett wracked his mind for a different angle, but Renton was fast concluding the brief. 'No, we have our tasks. Jump to it, laddie.' He strode to the door and held it open for Barrett.

'And...laddie, since you've been here I have not seen you with your service revolver...I'm guessing it's gone AWOL somewhere, so do make sure and draw one from the armoury, before you head up the line.'

Barrett nodded.

'Yes sir, will do,' he said, but the door had already been closed behind him.

-19-

Northern France, September 8th, 1917

14:30 hrs

For the third time, Barrett hinged the barrel of the Webley revolver forward, to reveal the hexagonal arrangement of rounds, their brass percussion caps all facing him. He had fired one of these antiques on a range, years ago. He remembered the thrill of the noise each shot had made; the kick of the revolver as it bucked his hand upwards; the acrid smell of cordite filling his nostrils. Shooting a target, back then, had been a rush, a boyhood fantasy. Never had he imagined that he may have to discharge one towards another human being. He snapped the barrel back up and pushed the revolver into its holster, taking care to fasten the flap over the top.

He was sat in the rear of a covered-over, horse-drawn cart, on a dusty road heading for the Ypres salient: the frontline trench network. On either side of him, two enormous redcap military policemen tended themselves in silence. One nibbled on a fingernail cuticle aimlessly, the other seemed to be constantly scratching here, there and everywhere, most likely lousy with fleas. Opposite, another two redcaps, slightly smaller in stature, but equally menacing; their faces set, uncompromising, ready for the task ahead, Barrett thought. Next to the open end of the cart, Smithers and Tomkinson sat facing each other. Most of the time looking out, as the cart trundled along, at the gradually increasing activity of life nearing the front. Now and then, the cart would pass a column of troops and someone would spy the corporals' yellow arm bands, invariably leading to a harsh cry of derision as they remembered, perhaps, their own spell in the Bull Ring.

Barrett could hear the growing volume of artillery fire, the din of men, animals and machines signifying nearing proximity to the war. The 'road' gradually turned from dust to mud, with great swirls and dug-in tracks making the cartwheels cavort wildly, as they tried to negotiate a straight path. The air itself seemed to become thicker - foggy somehow. Then, suddenly, the cart came to a halt. The two canaries, each carrying a slung Lee Enfield rifle, hopped over the rear edge; Barrett heard their boots squelch into the thick mud underfoot. Smithers glanced back at him.

'Walking from here on in, sir.' He said with an apathetic air.

Barrett followed suit. Within two minutes, the seven men were walking towards an opening, leading down into the ground: the entrance into the trench network. The path sloped downwards, and the men soon found themselves descending from ground level to a depth of fifteen feet. Wooden sleepers reinforced the mud walls which grew up on either side of them, as they passed through seemingly endless tributaries, following signs hammered in at various corners, showing painted place names that Barrett had seen in grainy, black and white photographs: Piccadilly, Charing Cross and Liverpool Street. The air was getting thicker as a dense mist continued to descend, blanketing the trenches, and everything within. It seemed to be laced with a dirty, acidic-tasting scent, and Barrett could hear men coughing; he wondered just how toxic the atmosphere was here.

With each turn, yet another trench stretched out ahead of them, constantly changing direction, many of them through ninety degrees – to limit explosion damage, Barrett remembered reading. All the time, the volume of the noise increased, but it wasn't just the sound that was intensifying. The tension in the air was palpable. As the group walked on, they had initially passed soldiers that had grimaced at the sight of the redcaps and canaries. One or two had 'accidentally' spat phlegm just ahead of their walking feet, followed quickly by a faux apology '...sorry sir, didn't see you there', or something similar. But the deeper they went, the closer they got to the front proper, the fierce looks tended to fade, not because their hatred of the Étaples staff lessened, no, that was still there. It was because their presence didn't mean anything to them. They were cannon fodder now, just the same, if fate so deemed it.

Some twenty minutes after entering the underground network, Barrett and his company arrived at a wider crossroads section, identified by a slightly larger sign, roughly painted with the words, 'Waterloo Junction'. Their arrival generated some scurry, ultimately bringing a grey-haired captain out from a side dugout, hatless, with crumbs of some indistinguishable foodstuffs stuck to his unkempt whiskers. He looked at Barrett and, with some disdain, the other men.

'Good morning,' he said, looking Barrett up and down. 'Your tidy uniform and your...' He glowered at the redcaps, '...companions, suggest that you are here to pick up my men.' His hands swept down the front of his jacket, seemingly conscious that he looked a good deal less 'tidy' than he would have liked. Barrett saluted, drawing a small titter from the nearby soldiers, keen to see what was going on.

'Yes sir, I have orders to collect five deserters for return to Étaples depot.' The captain flinched at the word 'deserters'. Barrett should have known better. He quickly regretted using the word. The captain looked at Barrett reproachfully.

'That's one word for them, I suppose. Another description would be, simply, men who have taken as much as they can; men who just couldn't go on.' Barrett wanted to apologise. What he, of course, knew was that the captain was describing the -- then unknown condition of -- post-traumatic stress disorder, or to use the colloquial term of the period, just beginning to emerge in general parlance: 'shell shock'. Before Barrett could say any more, however, the captain leaned against the wall, pulling a pack of woodbines from his trouser pocket.

145

'I'm afraid they're not here, old stick. We were pulled off the Line last night, ahead of schedule – wonders will never cease.' He motioned to the trench, off to his left, barely visible in the descending murk. 'They were left up there, in custody with the oncoming -- the Warwicks -- for some reason.' He offered a cigarette to Barrett and, when he declined, continued. 'It's not much farther on. About another fifteen minutes that way.' Barrett nodded his thanks, saluted once again, and made to move off. The captain called after him. 'Word of advice, old stick...' Barrett looked back as he walked, seeing the man point towards the trench sides. '...keep your head down, the walls are a little low in places.'

The captain was certainly correct. Eventually entering a trench marked by a sign that said: 'The Promenade', the seven men had to stoop, often very low indeed, where the trench wall had dipped – a casualty of random shell bombardment. The sappers were constantly repairing these revetments, normally in the hours of darkness, when the risk of sniper fire was a little lower. As they continued on, Barrett knew they were getting close, as he noticed the chained deer cap badge that signified the Royal Warwickshire Regiment. These men looked decidedly fresher than the ones Barrett had left, having just taken station along this part of the front. The level of readiness, however, was electric. At one point he noticed, with alarm, the gas mask bags hanging from all the soldiers' webbing.

Shit, that's something we don't have.

Seeing a sign that indicated the C.O.'s dugout, he glanced sideways at Smithers to tell him to stay put, while he paid his complements.

He never got the chance.

A neat round hole had suddenly appeared in the centre of the canary's forehead. An instant later, the sound of a single shot caught up, and Smithers, his uninterested-looking expression frozen on his face for all time, fell backwards into the mud.

The trench erupted.

Spinning around, Barrett looked up to see one or two muzzle flashes *inside the trench,* as bullets zipped past his face and body. Beyond the flashes, in amongst the puffs of gun smoke, and just barely, through the dense, cloying fog, he glimpsed a different colour uniform: the field grey of German infantry.

Holy shit... Barrett thought, as the slow-motion scene played out before him.

He began reaching for his revolver, inwardly cursing himself for securing it so tightly under the holster flap, when he was tackled to the ground from behind. As his face buried into the mud, he was conscious of a sharp pain, spearing up his back. He tried to move but the weight lying across him had other ideas. It was one of the M.P.s, one of the brutes he'd sat next to in the cart. He was pretty certain the policeman had just saved his life, for which he would be very grateful, if he managed to get out of this alive. The gratitude very quickly began turning to panic, however, as the big man's immobility started to make Barrett feel pinned down, trapped. Trying to wriggle free, the shots continued to pass by, very closely. Unlike countless films he'd seen, the bullets did not ricochet off things with that satisfying 'peeeyow' sound. Instead, spots of mud sporadically splashed his face, as the rounds cut deep into the dirt-clay mixture of the wall. This was indication enough just how close death was. Barrett tried to crawl forward, but the M.P. was taking his close protection a little too far.

Unmoving. Unyielding.

'For Christ's sake, get off me, or we've all had it.' He shouted over the cacophony. No movement. Biting down on his lower lip, Barrett realised the man was dead, that or knocked unconscious by something – though there had been no explosions. Yet.

The gunfire continued on. Barrett dug his elbows deep, trying to drag himself forward, fighting the deadweight on his back and the treacle-like mud, each movement squelching and sucking him down, resisting his attempts.

Mission Fail, he thought fleetingly. *I'm going to die here.*

Bizarrely, in the moments before he knew must be the end, all he could concentrate on was the horrible, clay taste of the sludge in his mouth. It had strangely become an imperative that he swilled his mouth with fresh water from his canteen. He wondered if he had the strength to dig it out, where, along with his revolver holster, it too had become buried between the French mud and the dead M.P., lying over him.

Then.

Closer.

Shots with a different report.

He couldn't see, but he could hear; the new sound came from behind him.

A counterattack.

A heavy boot stamped on his left hand. It wasn't painful, it simply pushed his hand deeper into the mud. But the boot was brown, topped with tightly wound puttees. A Tommy!

The return fire quickly became effective. The British soldiers passed Barrett's still prone body, on their way down the trench, repelling the German attack. He struggled doggedly to unglue himself from the sucking filth, managing to grab a piece of timber in the sidewall. By the time he had pulled himself upright, it appeared to be all over. The enemy had been suppressed, at least as far as he could see. He felt a hand grip his arm below the elbow. He looked round into the face of Tomkinson; no longer confidant, no longer intimidating. The corporal's eyes were dewy, wet with tears. He looked unhurt; in fact, he looked pristine: no splashes of mud, his revolver, just like Barrett's, still in its holster.

No. Not like Barrett's.

Tomkinson looked as if he'd been somewhere else, throughout the encounter. Barrett looked down at himself; the entire front of his uniform, head-to-toe, was caked in grey-brown mud. Around him: carnage. To join Smithers and the big redcap, two of the other M.P.s had also been hit. One of these was dead, several gaping wounds through his torso; the other, the second large redcap, sat on a sandbag, holding his jaw, blood pouring like water from a tap, through the man's fingers. Barrett pointed Tomkinson towards the M.P.

'See what you can do there,' he said.

Tomkinson simply stared back, eyes wide and frightened. He didn't move.

'Tear off some cloth from something; try to stem his bleeding, man!'

Tomkinson was frozen still. Barrett wondered whether to shout at him, to try to galvanize him into action, but then thought better of it. Words were useless, he realised. He wiped his filthy hands as best he could and crouched down next to the redcap.

'Alright, take it easy. Help is on its way.' He looked around for something to act as a bandage. There was nothing. Up close, the man's wound looked far worse. His jawbone jutted out of the side of one cheek, splintered, sharp and brilliant white against the dark red. He was losing blood at a rapid rate. Barrett knew that the injury was survivable, but the blood loss...that was the problem. He began unfastening the redcap's jacket, hoping the man wore a vest underneath that he could rip strips from. He worked fast, pulling the buttons open, yanking the jacket wide. No joy. A thick, fleecy pullover lay beneath.

This won't work, he thought despairingly. He turned back to Tomkinson.

'Hey..hey' He yelled. 'Are you wearing a vest?' The corporal gave a robotic nod. 'Strip it off, fast - I need some kind of dressing here.' For a moment, Barrett wondered if this was asking too much, but then, with surprising swiftness, Tomkinson began to pull his jacket buttons undone. Barrett turned back to the M.P.

'It's going to be alright; I'm going to get...' He stopped.

The M.P. looked back, *through him.* Eyes glazed over. His pallor told Barrett all he needed to know.

How could he have died that fast?

Barrett slumped back on his haunches.

-20-

Northern France, September 8th, 1917

18:00 hrs

Barrett's head broke the surface of the steaming hot water and he breathed in the cool air. His eyes slowly opened, blinking several times to ward off the moisture, temporarily blurring his vision. He'd been submerged only for a few seconds, but for that miniscule moment he had the feeling of being disembodied, distant, away from this living nightmare. It was a welcome feeling.

I want to go home.

His mind wandered back to the aftermath of the trench raid. He had been guided into the C.O.'s dugout, where a private had brought him a hot cup of tea to accompany the two or three swigs of brandy from the resident regiment lieutenant's hip flask. He vaguely remembered the officer explaining how these raids had become more commonplace; how they had once been a feature of night activity only. It seemed that the misty conditions and poor visibility had provided an opportunity too good to miss. The young lieutenant had also suggested that the Germans may have had some espionage-insight as to the planned handover between off going and oncoming regiments. The usual confusion of this exchange would have been the ideal time to strike. Fortunately, for most anyway, the handover had happened earlier than scheduled - the night before. A blessing really; the Warwicks had managed to have a little time to become embedded - enough time to provide a capable repel. As far as Barrett's ill fortune, however...

'Just a case of the wrong place, at the wrong time, I'm afraid.' The lieutenant had said in a slightly blasé tone, seemingly uninformed of the loss of three of Barrett's party. As Barrett had begun to regain some calm, he thought he would get the shakes. He'd had them before. On this occasion, they didn't come. At least, not yet.

After a while, he had re-joined Tomkinson and the other two redcaps, who had busied themselves organising collection of the five deserters. The prisoners looked mercifully thankful to be leaving the trench system – that being their intent all along, of course. Even the one missing some toes, made fairly rapid progress on two roughly made crutches. No-one spoke on the return journey. Tomkinson had stared vacantly into space. Barrett didn't know what he was thinking, but neither did he much care at that moment. The detainees were silent; Barrett judged they must have known that it was their retrieval that had resulted in the death of yet more men.

Eventually, they arrived back in camp. Their appearance, particularly Barrett's, had drawn some enquiring looks from the gate guards. He'd disembarked the cart, leaving the administrative processing to Tomkinson, and had walked the remaining distance back to the Officers' Mess, where the ever-present Mess steward had wasted no time in drawing Barrett a hot bath. The corporal had asked no questions, had made no comment, and Barrett had inwardly been grateful for the steward's discretionary professionalism. The brick of carbolic soap had struggled to remove the grime and caked-in blood at first, but persistence and the almost unbearably hot water had helped. He had eventually been satisfied that he'd scrubbed it all away, but as he pulled on some fresh uniform, he cursed himself as he saw some remnant of red down the sides of his thumbnails.

Later that evening, Barrett sat in the Mess at dinner. He had seen neither Sumner nor Renton since he'd returned from the front. His enquiries as to Renton's whereabouts had drawn blanks from everyone he'd spoken to. It appeared whatever his 'business' was, it had been a solitary affair. Pushing his half-eaten meal away, he was preparing to return to his room when he spied Sumner walking past the dining room doors. He waved, trying to get the young man's attention, feeling sure the second lieutenant had seen him, but whether he had or not, he walked on.

What now? Barrett wondered, rising from the table, in pursuit. Barrett caught up to him just as he was opening his room door.

'Lionel.' He called, causing Sumner, at last, to stop and turn around. He looked dreadful, Barrett thought. His eyes were red rimmed, standing out against a pasty white skin pallor that reminded Barrett oddly of cold porridge. Barrett saw something else too in the poorly lit corridor. Sumner's hands were gently shaking. The young lieutenant offered a feeble smile.

'Oh...hello Liam.' He said in a very quiet voice. Barrett reached out a hand and gently held the young man's shoulder.

'Well, I thought *I'd* had a lousy day, but you look terrible. What have you been doing?' He had to admit, it wasn't that he was particularly interested, but the look on the man's face, coupled with the mystery of his 'special duty' had made him curious. Sumner shrugged his shoulders, staring down towards his feet.

'Yeah, I'm sorry, but I *have* had a pretty abysmal day, actually; please...I hope you don't mind; I'd rather not talk about it.'

He won't look me in the eye. Barrett thought.

Sumner continued to turn in towards his room and Barrett considered briefly whether to push for an explanation. He thought better of it and offered a reassuring smile.

'OK. Let's talk tomorrow eh?'

Sumner, nodded gratefully, slowly closing the door behind him.

It's probably just as well Barrett thought. *I have some work to do.*

A quick detour into his room, to pick up his cap and a greatcoat, and Barrett was back out into the rapidly falling dusk. Pulling the collar up on the enormous coat, he headed straight for the B-Comp. staff building. Passing by the camp tents and marquees on his way, he could hear the activity of the day winding down. Men milled around, most sitting on the ground -- exhausted from the day's energy-sapping concoction of 'training exercises' -- smoking and chatting quietly. The failing light concealed him for the most part, and he rarely had to return a salute. This was just fine for what Barrett wanted to achieve.

The staff building was in darkness as he approached, as expected. He let himself in through the entrance door, which was not secured, but wasn't surprised to then find Renton's door locked up tight. Having no pick lock equipment, he briefly considered forcing the door, then had another idea. Retracing his steps back outside, he edged his way around the perimeter wall, finding Renton's window. At just over chest height, he reached up and teased his fingers underneath the corner of the window, pulling gently. It gave outwards a little, under the pressure he applied, but then caught on the latch. Barrett scanned around the grass and small bushes, finding a suitably thin, but long, twig. Cautiously, he pushed the twig in through the gap he'd made between the window and frame, and slowly, taking care not to break the brittle stick, eased the latch upwards from its hasp. Giving a last look around to make sure no-one was nearby, he pulled himself up and into Renton's office.

Inside, Barrett made a quick search of the captain's desk; the drawers were unlocked but revealed nothing of interest. He hadn't thought anything would be there. Renton was too savvy to leave anything obviously incriminating for Major Davenport to stumble across. In any case, when he'd been in the office earlier that morning – seemingly, a thousand years ago – he had noticed a large filing cabinet in the corner. Nothing unusual in that, but this one, he had noticed, had a thick metal bar covering the front of the drawers, fastened at the top by a large, robust-looking padlock; and that, Barrett had decided, *did* look out of place. Barrett stood for a moment, regarding the bar and padlock. The cabinet was not like the old metal monstrosities that had pre-dated digital records; this one was of wooden construction and, though the bar and padlock were pretty impregnable, the cabinet itself was less so. As quietly as he could, Barrett swivelled the cabinet around, pivoting it on one corner, to expose its rear wall. Peering around the office for a suitable tool, he saw Renton's field webbing, hanging on a coat stand in the corner, including, in its long scabbard, his bayonet. The blade was huge, at least 40 centimetres long, Barrett estimated.

Talk about a sledgehammer to crack a nut.

Despite its size, it proved to be perfect. Prying the wooden back panel apart, with the point of the weapon, he was able to easily push the blade down, its widening girth levering the panel away readily, pulling the brad pins out, through the wood, quietly and effectively. In two minutes, the whole rear panel was off, gently laid against the office wall. Barrett began at the top of the cabinet, pulling each drawer out, rearwards, then lifted carefully down to the floor for a closer look. The increasing darkness was making visibility difficult now. He estimated he only had perhaps fifteen more minutes and the office would be pitch black.

The first drawer had revealed nothing. Just paperwork related to the work at Étaples. Similarly, the second also looked worthlessly mundane. Pulling out the third, penultimate drawer, the unmistakable sound of footfalls on gravel made him freeze. The sound was just outside the window and Barrett fought the urge to peek out. He waited, crouched on the floor, trying desperately to steady his breathing. In the dark silence, he could hear the *swish swash* of his heartbeat in his ears and foolishly wondered whether it was just as audible to others. The footsteps seemed to be steadily receding. He wanted to wait until they'd gone completely, but he knew he just didn't have time, not if he wished to see things adequately. At the bottom of the drawer was a small strong box. No way he could crack that, he thought; however, just as he was about to give up and repack what he'd disturbed, a manila folder slipped from his hand, spilling its contents onto the floor. Gathering the papers up he could see that they were requisition documents. Lots of them.

This is it, he thought, casting his mind back to Renton and Davenport's eavesdropped conversation.

'...profiteering from black marketed medical supplies...'

Barrett strained his eyes, but he could barely see the words, the light was getting just too dim. Time was up. He folded half a dozen of the documents and secreted them into his tunic, underneath his breast pocket, then quickly stashed the remainder back into the folder. It took him five minutes and he'd pressed the back panel of the cabinet back into place; it wasn't perfect, but moving the cabinet back against the wall, he hoped, would conceal any obvious disturbance.

Gently lowering himself down to the ground, he eased the window back into place. He couldn't properly close it, of course, but then again, it hadn't been fully shut before. He paused and peered at the ground in the semi-darkness, making sure he hadn't left any obvious footprints. Contented with his handiwork, he turned back towards the front of the building, just in time to see a dark shape emerging from the bushes to his side. Turning to see what the shape was, he had no time to react before something hard struck him squarely on the front of the jaw. No pain. No blinding light, just black oblivion.

-21-

Northern France, September 8th, 1917

21:30 hrs

Barrett crawled slowly back to consciousness, vaguely aware of a mumbling conversation, somewhere off to his left. Something else he was only too aware of was pain, searing pain, coming from his jaw. He tried to exercise his mouth open and closed, and immediately regretted it. Involuntarily sucking in air through his teeth, he murmured aloud in half suppressed agony. Attempting to reach a hand up to feel whether his jaw was, in fact, still there, he found he was unable to move his arms at all. His wrists had been bound behind his back. Tilting his head towards the direction of the conversation, he struggled to focus, making out two figures, some four or five metres away in the gloom. They were sat at a table, either side of a lit candle, like two lovers in a romantic restaurant. Barrett's utterance of pain had alerted them; they had ceased talking and were now looking his way. As he sat, orientating himself to the environment, it occurred to him how his senses were returning, one by one. Hearing first, followed by touch -- well, pain at any rate -- then sight, and now, finally, smell. And this last came across with the most intensity. It was a fetid aroma, not unlike a laundry basket; a musty dankness. Slowly, his eyes grew accustomed to the dark; he realised he was in some kind of cave.

One of the figures rose from the table and walked over, coming into view. It was Renton.

'You're heavier than you look, laddie.' He said, a slight smile on his lips. He stood before the bound captive, hands on his hips, slowly shaking his head like a disappointed father addressing a wayward son. 'I'm sorry about the whack. But I'm afraid that might only be the beginning.'

A harsh voice interrupted him: the other cave dweller. *Bad cop?* Barrett wondered.

'Don't mollycoddle him, Al. You shouldn't have even brought him here.' The second figure came to stand beside Renton; a full foot shorter, wearing shabby-looking civilian clothes, his unkempt appearance suggested he'd been living in this cave for some considerable time, Barrett thought, between the waves of throbbing. Renton's smile vanished instantly as he turned his wrath towards the smaller man.

'Shut your trap. I told you why it was necessary.'

Of course, Barrett pondered, *you need to know whether I'm working with anyone...* Renton lowered his voice once again, speaking calmly as if the anger hadn't surfaced at all. Barrett was becoming accustomed to Renton's swift and short-lived swings of mood. 'Now...why don't you just bugger off and leave things to me.'

The civilian shrugged uncaringly, turning on his heel.

'Fine. Just know though: if you don't sort it, I will.'

Barrett detected a no-nonsense tone in how this simple statement was delivered; there was a clear difference here to that of Renton's canary toadies. It was obvious that this man was more of an equal partner in their relationship, someone who couldn't easily be manipulated. He suspected that Renton held sway *for now*, but the certainty in the voice made Barrett wonder how long that arrangement would last. The man strode from the cave while Renton dragged a chair across, sitting astride it backwards, his arms hugging the seat back.

'Liam, Liam, Liam...' He uttered in a fatherly tone. He tipped his head back briefly in the direction where the civilian had left. '...you know what my colleague thinks, I gather?' Barrett nodded slowly. If he had any chance of escaping this, it had to be through Renton. His mind raced. He'd used the word 'colleague' rather than 'friend', could he work on that? Probably not, he thought miserably. Renton went on.

'So, what to do with you.' He reached inside his jacket, pulling out the requisition dockets that Barrett had taken such great pains to obtain. 'It appears that you're onto us...' leafing through the pages '...if it were up to my colleague, you'd be dead already.' He stopped briefly to look Barrett in the eye. 'How am I to prevent that happening?' He asked, searchingly. There was something in the way he asked the question that made Barrett feel he was genuinely sincere. *Why wasn't he dead already?* Renton looked down into his lap with a dejected hang of the head. 'The bottom line is, I need you to start talking, laddie. I need you to tell me everything or...' He looked at Barrett imploringly, leaving the sentence hanging in the air.

163

He doesn't even want to say it, Barrett thought. *He wants to be merciful.* The reason for this? God only knew, but for a certainty, Barrett felt that if he could just give him a glimmer of an explanation.

In that moment, Barrett made up his mind which direction to take. It was a gamble, of course. The risk of a bullet in the back of the brain stem was difficult to ignore, but he had to give it his best try. He'd only known Renton for a few short days, but he believed, in that time, he had assessed his 'profile' enough to have a decent chance of manipulating the outcome. In any case, if he got it wrong, he wouldn't need to dwell on it for long.

He started to talk.

'You don't need to put the thumb screws on me.' Barrett said with a croaking voice. Renton walked briefly back to the table, bringing a glass back and touching it to Barrett's lips. The smell and taste of the wine fought against overriding pain as Barrett slurped down a small mouthful. Some of the liquid trickled down his chin, though he didn't feel it. He tried again to speak, this time with a little more success.

'I *could* tell you that I am just one part of a team, tasked with bringing a ring of bootleggers to justice.'

He noticed Renton wrinkle his nose slightly; he clearly didn't like the term 'bootlegger' nor, quite obviously, did he see himself as one. Barrett went on.

'I *could* tell you that we have had suspicions for a while now; knowledge of how 'supplies' have been disappearing, equipment: unaccounted for.' He paused to give his jaw a slight rest before continuing.

'I *could* tell you of how I was selected to infiltrate your network, to find evidence of your involvement – which I now have. I *could* tell you that part of the mission was to also, if possible, uncover the rest of your cell, so that they too could be brought to account. I could also tell you that my team is aware of exactly what, where and when I was doing things and that, should I not report in, the cavalry would be immediately dispatched to swoop down on you, charging you not only with illegal holding and distribution of military materiel, but now...' he paused again, weighing the final word, for impact, '...murder.'

Renton had sat back down on the chair. He swallowed a little of the wine he had offered Barrett. Staring at his prisoner. Contemplating. He nodded back towards his prisoner.

'You keep using the word 'could' in all of this. What do you mean? Imagining for a minute that your story is true, are you telling me that you could be dissuaded from doing all that you've said? Is that what you're implying?'

It was Barrett's turn to smile, though he was fairly certain he did not have the muscular control to achieve this feat. The result was more of a grimace. Instead, he simply shook his head.

'No. All these things I could have said, *may* have been useful in securing myself some temporary safety...' he nodded towards the exit of the cave. '...as you've said, your colleague has already decided I am a dead man. I *could have* banked on you erring on the side of caution – choosing imprisonment instead of the gallows.'

Renton's face showed confusion; he placed the glass down on the earthen floor.

'So what *are* you saying, laddie?' Leaning forward, gripping the seat back with both hands. Barrett took a deep breath before continuing – this was it.

'I'm saying it's all a lie.' He paused again, briefly.

'I am *not* part of an investigation into what you're doing. I'm simply saying that I could have run with this, to try to delay you killing me.' He paused yet again; he needed desperately for Renton to piece things together himself, for this to have any chance of success. Renton spread his hands out in a questioning manner, as if to ask: So? Barrett went on, slowly.

'This morning...God, it seems so long ago now...the meeting with Davenport...' he waited for Renton to nod. 'I listened in at the door after we'd been dismissed.' Renton sneered slightly at this, and Barrett nearly laughed there and then at the absurdity of thinking that eavesdropping was the biggest crime on trial here.

'Go on.' Renton said.

'I heard your argument...but I also heard him accuse you of...well...' he glanced at the documents that Renton had thrown on the floor. '...this.' He tried to lean forwards, but the ropes had also fastened him to the chair, as well as binding his hands. 'I needed to know it was true...it sounded equally possible that Davenport was just making false accusations...especially as it seems clear to me that you have him over a barrel...' He paused, trying to judge the impact he was having. Renton gave a slight, almost imperceptible nod.

'That snivelling shit has hidden out in soft jobs and backwaters this entire war. His turn is coming, believe me...' another sneer. '...I've seen to it.' He pondered for a moment, rubbing his chin, before continuing. 'It's true, he did surprise me this morning; I didn't believe he'd have the nous to look into my dealings -- I guess a man will try most things to save his bacon.' With this he looked back at Barrett, a mischievous smile on his lips. 'Is that what you're doing now, laddie? Trying to save your bacon?' Not waiting for an answer, he went on. 'I can't say it bothers me. By the time he's in a position to do anything about it, he'll be staring down the barrels of a whole load of German Mausers.'

Barrett fidgeted on the chair, trying to find a new position. He glanced up, showing discomfort.

'Any chance you can untie me from the chair, at least?' He asked.

Renton smiled.

'Not a chance. Go on, I'm enjoying this.'

Barrett relaxed his muscles against the panic urge to thrash around against the ropes. He consciously sighed out, composing himself.

'Look. I am not ashamed of my situation here; if I'm to go back to the Line, then so be it; if you're going to finish me off, here and now...well...there's bugger all I can do about that either...' He uttered this in an 'I'm-angry-with-the-world' manner, rather than begging for mercy, a tactic he felt might be more agreeable to Renton's own outlook. 'Am I afraid? You bet your fucking life I am, but I'll not do a Davenport and hide under a fucking sandbag. As far as I'm concerned, I've already spilled blood for the King...I know you have too. I also know that when this is all done and dusted, people like you and me will be ignored in the street.' Barrett could see Renton leaning forward again; he'd stopped smiling.

'As you said when we first met, yes, I *had* been wallowing around back home. My wounds took a long time to heal, but what hurt more...far more...was the way people looked at me. It wasn't a white feather thing; they could see I was convalescing. No, it was something else. At the start of the war, things were different. When you were medevacked home, after Mons, it was all brand new, all novel and patriotic; people were still proud of what we were doing...'

Renton held a hand up in interruption.

'Medevacked?' he said, eyebrow raised.

Barrett cursed himself. The anachronism had crept in while he was in full Oscar-winning mode. He shook his head impatiently, moving on swiftly.

'Errr, medically evacuated, it's a phrase they are bandying around in the hospitals now.' He quickly went on. 'The point is: before Kitchener had to start drafting men in, before our noses had been bloodied a few times, everything was accepted. We were all fighting for a good cause...we were all considered...heroes!'

Was Renton nodding?

'But now...three years on and no nearer the end? The public...the people...they just want it done.' He could see Renton's expression changing. This was not news to him, Barrett thought. He was casting out in the right place.

Just have to land it, now.

'When it does finally end...' he looked imploringly into Renton's eyes. '...and provided we're still alive, that is, our homecoming will not be like your last one.' He paused again. Letting each sentence hit home. 'Trust me, we will have fought, bled and died...and for what? A pittance of pension and the sneer of a...' he searched for the right example, '...a fucking bookmaker, or a bank clerk...or...I dunno what.'

Barrett went quiet. Renton did not look at him for a full minute, but eventually, he lifted up his gaze. And Barrett was waiting.

'I want in, sir.'

It was late. The estaminet was virtually empty, save for the two men, sat opposite one another, and the waiter -- who Barrett determined was probably also the owner -- sitting quietly by the bar, willing his last two patrons to wrap up. Two empty bottles of wine sat on the table between the men, with a third being held in Renton's large paw hands, as he fiddled with the label, trying to peel it off cleanly. The alcohol had finally put to rest the last of the stabbing pain in Barrett's jaw. He acknowledged inwardly that he was a little inebriated; it would have been far worse had he not made the subtle effort of drinking one glass to Renton's three. He savoured the fresh night air, consciously grateful of how close he'd come to never breathing it again. Renton had bought into his tale. Of sorts.

The civilian, who'd turned out not to be a civilian at all, but Private Stanley Jones, the name Davenport had threatened Renton with, was a long-time-hunted deserter. He had returned some time later, along with a swarthy pair of equally absconding, renegade ex-squaddies to, no doubt, make the nosey lieutenant disappear. As expected, Jones had not been enamoured with the idea that Barrett could be trusted, and a lengthy argument had ensued between the two men. Renton had pulled Jones to the side of the cave, away from Barrett, to obviously explain exactly how his faith was justified. The majority of the discussion, Barrett didn't hear clearly, but what little he could was replete with obscenities, mainly from Jones. One thing Barrett did hear plainly, was a promise from Renton:

'If it comes to that, I'll end the bastard myself!'

Fair enough. Barrett had mused.

Though Barrett found the whole dishonourable venture despicable in itself, Renton would never know how minor this entire affair was, to the detective's real mission. In any event, it seemed that he had now been recruited into the team of bootleggers – all the better for allowing him the access to Renton that he needed in the days ahead. And so, some few hours later, they had found themselves back in the town, with Renton toasting -- again and again -- their newly cemented partnership.

Renton finally abandoned the bottle label and poured the last dribble of wine into his own glass. Barrett was exhausted. This had truly been a day without end. He wanted sleep so badly, but after the reprieve he'd secured, he felt it imperative to validate Renton's trust in him, with a few 'drinkies' to seal the deal. Renton slugged back the wine and staggered to his feet.

'Come along then,' he said, banging his leg into the table, sending glasses clattering. The two men started the slow stumble back to camp. After some minutes had passed, Renton spoke, very quietly, as if masking his voice from would-be spies.

'Jones doesn't like you Liam...says I'm too gullible.' He slurred his S's, as he opened up, the booze freeing up any earlier reservations. Barrett felt it best not to try to defend himself. After tonight, his persuasion 'quotient' was empty. Fortunately, Renton didn't require a conversation. He went on. 'I heard what happened to you today.' He reached an arm across Barrett's shoulders for a good old man hug. 'One of the M.P.s told me; said you'd all had it bloody rough, like...'

So, not Tomkinson then.

As if Renton had heard Barrett's thoughts, he carried on, with some bitterness.

'That idiot Tomkinson has checked himself into the hospital...fuckin' fairy...a little bit of action and he's running for his Mammy...' He dissolved into giggles at his own evaluation. 'Too many fuckin' queers around here anyway, if you ask me...'

Nice. Barrett pondered. *A pathological nutcase and homophobic to boot,* Barrett thought, though he knew this to be a common derogatory term for the period. He wasn't really surprised by Tomkinson's actions, but he wondered exactly how the corporal had managed to admit himself under the banner of battle stress, after one short encounter, when men were going through far worse, each and every day, not ten miles distant.

A thought occurred to Barrett as they crossed the veranda into the Mess entrance. Renton wasn't exactly surrounded with allies. Davenport was clearly the enemy; Smithers was dead, Tomkinson hadn't covered himself in glory, after today's incident. That left Lyman, Jones and his gang of miscreants...and him: Liam Barrett. He began to realise why his story had been accepted. Renton clearly wasn't a man who *needed* friends, that much was obvious, but neither could he proceed completely alone. As he turned toward his room, Renton gripped his elbow. Cryptically saying with a wink.

'Get some good kip, laddie. Things are going to be interesting tomorrow, wait and see.'

Barrett smiled back wanly, remembering the date of the 'Mutiny at Étaples.'

You don't know the half of it sunshine.

-22-

Northern France, September 9th, 1917

10:30 hrs

Barrett sat back behind his desk, lifting the welcome steaming mug of tea to his lips that Simmons had silently brought in. He'd just completed a briefing of two replacement canaries, seconded from A and C Companies, to replace Smithers and Tomkinson. Simmons had earlier given him a titbit of information that the latter had 'gone stark staring mad' in the hospital, after the doctor on duty had essentially told him there was nothing wrong with him, and that he had to report back on duty. The briefing had been exactly that: brief. After all, the new men were to be employed doing the same job as before, simply in a slightly different part of camp. Barrett pondered whether to tell them to be on their guard today, but then decided against it. It wasn't like he could give them a reason. Similarly, though Anders had assured him that events didn't change all that much – *his bloody umbrella theory* – he still felt that it was potentially dangerous to be actively making alterations that could affect the timeline.

He pushed himself back in his chair, rubbing at the dull ache that still persisted where his jaw reached under his right ear. He desperately needed more sleep. He had buried his head deep into his pillow when he'd heard the bugle sound reveille much earlier and had grabbed two more hours 'shut-eye', banking on Renton doing likewise. Sure enough, when he had made it into the staff room, he had found Davenport hopping mad, demanding to know where everyone was. He wasn't even aware of Smithers' death, having clearly not bothered to read the sketched-out report Barrett had made the day before. He assumed that the major was more annoyed by the fact that Renton hadn't turned in yet. Barrett had found Sumner 'brewing up' in the canteen and had tried to thank him for 'holding the fort', but, just like the evening before, he hadn't been keen for conversation. The young man looked beaten, defeated. It *had* to have been his 'special duty'...

What the hell had that been?

He hadn't been given the chance to enquire further before the two new canaries were waiting outside his office, having been pushed down the chain of command by Davenport. Eyeing the threadbare lounge chair in the corner of his office, wondering whether it would be comfortable enough for a mid-morning snooze, the door opened wide, with Renton filling the opening, a wide grin on his face. In his hands, he held a large buff envelope, still sealed, Barrett noted.

'Morning laddie. I hope you slept well. I know I did.' He held the envelope so that Barrett could make out the writing on the front. It read:

175

'OIC B-Company, Classified, Immediate attention required'

Barrett looked back at Renton; his expression was one of pure glee.

'You can stand outside, or you can come in, I'll leave that up to you; but either way, I'm going to enjoy this.' He motioned Barrett to follow as he walked on down to Davenport's office. Rather than the knock, and wait to be admitted, Renton pushed the door open and walked straight in. Barrett chose to linger in the corridor, suspecting what was about to happen.

'What the bloody hell...' Davenport's voice could be heard clearly, still trying in vain to maintain an air of superiority, *even after Renton had floored him yesterday,* Barrett mused.

'Oh, be quiet, you bloody idiot.' Renton's harsh return. 'Here, there's something in the post for you.' Barrett heard the envelope hit the desk with a soft thud, scattering a pot of pencils in a noisy clatter. Barrett peeked through the gap of the door jamb, seeing Davenport standing there, behind his desk, alternately looking from Renton to the envelope. Renton continued.

'Don't kid yourself, Davenport, we both know what it says. I warned you...did you honestly think I would go back on my word?'

Davenport reached forward and picked up the envelope, tearing open one end and pulling out the contained document. His eyes feverishly read down the page, the redness in his cheeks visibly abating to a dull white. He looked back up into Renton's taunting eyes. Renton didn't need to say anything else; he could have left it at that, but he was clearly relishing the major's pain.

'Know what 'Immediate Effect' means, Davenport? It means right-fucking-now...'

Barrett could see Davenport's hands clenching into fists.

'...you'll be happy to know that I have kindly arranged an escort for you; two redcaps are waiting in the lobby...just to make sure you don't get lost...'

Davenport's previously bloodless white face was quickly colouring into a wrathful red.

'...I mean, it's not out of the question that you could take a wrong turn...seeing as you've never fucking been there...'

With surprising speed, Davenport launched himself out from behind his desk, but not towards Renton; the much smaller, older man would have stood no chance, even with rage on his side. Instead, his goal was his webbing, hanging on a hook in the corner, attached to which: his service revolver. Though he reached this rapidly, he fumbled with the holster flap, giving Renton all the time in the world to do something. But, oddly, the captain didn't move. In slow motion, Barrett saw the scene unravelling.

Was this to be Renton's murder...right in front of him?

Davenport had succeeded in extracting the weapon and, holding it two-handed, pulled back the cocking lever. Renton still remained motionless, seemingly awaiting his fate. Pivoting around, Davenport brought the pistol up to head height for the shot. The look in his eyes signified the intent. This was no idle threat. This was murder.

Barrett's shoulder hit the major's body at his waist, the two men cannoning into the wall with the force only a fully committed rugby tackle can deliver. The revolver spat fire, the bullet missing Renton's head by mere centimetres, impacting the wall behind, on its way through, befittingly, a framed certificate of Davenport's promotion to the rank of major. The noise of the shot was deafening in the small space of the office. Barrett's hearing was temporarily rendered useless; he could hear nothing save the strange, ringing after effect that a loud sound makes, yet, as he wrestled the gun from Davenport's hands, he managed a quick glance up at Renton, who even now, stood stock still. The captain was looking down at the writhing figures, grinning like a Cheshire cat, and Barrett reckoned -- if only he could hear it -- he'd be chuckling. In another ten seconds, the two waiting redcaps from the lobby had arrived and, after some barked instructions from Renton, were manhandling the major out of the door, presumably to the guard room cells. Barrett remained sitting on the floor for a moment, wiggling a finger in one ear in an effort to, somehow, restore normal function. A large, paw-hand appeared before his face and he looked up into the smiling face of Renton, offering to help him up.

Some hours later, on the other side of camp, Corporal William Ward of the 4th Gordon Highlanders stood, leaning on a fence, talking to a WAAC who happened to have been walking by. A little chit-chat with a pretty girl was a welcome relief to all the 'square-bashing' in the Bull Ring; any opportunity had to be grasped. Chat. That's all it was; that's all it could be. Non-commissioned ranks were banned from leaving the camp grounds, preventing any hope of a romantic assignation in the nearby town. With the exception of Lady Forbes' charity canteen, dishing out cups of tea and the odd hard tack biscuit to the troops, the only other chance of even *seeing* a female was if you were sent to the hospital. Mid conversation, the girl glanced down the road and could see an approaching redcap. Knowing the rules, she nervously made ready to leave. Ward too saw the policeman but wasn't as eager to move on, especially as, unusually, the policeman happened to be a private. Redcap or not, Ward deliberated, a corporal trumped a private, every day of the week.

The redcap in question was Private Harry Reece, recently deployed to Étaples depot. Reece was a confident, bullish man who usually made people see things his way with his fists. As a champion boxer in civilian life, he had no qualms about standing up to squaddies, even if they were, as was the case here, one of the notoriously battle-hardened Scottish regiment types. Since arriving, he had been itching to get 'in amongst 'em', especially those flippant Aussies that walked about the place, *calling us Poms!* As he approached the chatting couple, he felt his body begin to tense up.

He ain't even moving on...he can see me coming...cheeky bleeder. He thought.

Still some thirty feet away, Reece shouted out.

'Right, you two, you know the score; Jock: no fraternising.'

Ward turned his head towards Reece, but otherwise made no movement to disperse.

'We are just having a quick word...' Ward said, making an overly conspicuous effort to look at Reece's arms and shoulders, '...private.'

Incensed, Reece reached forward to spin the Highlander round. Ward had half expected this and was prepared for it. His fists started to rise in combative stance.

Excellent Reece thought. *Time to hand out a lesson. He can't know who I am...if he did, he'd...*

His thought, such as it was, ended there as the Highlander's rock-hard fist connected with Reece's jaw. It was enough to put the champion boxer on the ground, a feat no-one had managed to do in many recent fights in the ring. Perhaps it was this that spawned the following action. Perhaps the humiliation of the great Harold Reece being put on his backside...in front of a woman...was the reason that he jumped quickly to his feet, pulled his Webley revolver from its holster, and shot the Scottish corporal twice: one of the rounds, going into his head.

This was the start.

News travelled fast.

While Reece escaped through a known break in the wire, hoping for sanctuary in Étaples town, he knew that his actions could never be seen in any light, other than hot-blooded retaliatory murder. At the same time, the WAAC continued to scream for help, so hard, in fact, that she made her voice deeply hoarse and other worldly, only evident much later when she tried to explain what had happened. Ward had been stretchered to hospital fairly swiftly, but he never regained consciousness and died shortly afterwards. The news cascaded down through nurses, medics, orderlies and porters. It reached the troops, training in the Bull Ring, it reached those on the rifle range, it reached those in the gas mask training facility, those in the depots, the messes, the yards...everywhere.

The news spread like a contagion.

Within fifty minutes of the shooting, a New Zealand trooper stood on a wooden crate before a growing crowd of fellow Kiwis, Australians and Scots soldiers, rabble rousing with an ability that any self-respecting dockyard shop steward would have been proud. For some while now the Australian and New Zealand contingent of troops at Étaples had been protesting over the barbaric methods routinely and daily administered by the canaries and redcaps. Much of this unrest stemmed from the colonial soldiers' relative position of disciplinary safety; the death penalty, for example, could not be levelled at these soldiers, unlike their British counterparts.

The Kiwi soldier, atop the orange box, knew his audience well, knew exactly which buttons to press. The majority of training staff, indeed, the majority of British military command and control, was English, not British...English. A coincidently tragic comparison of this was evident: Reece, an Englishman, murdering Ward, a Scot. The inflammatory accusation was levelled: 'you Jocks are all being bullied by your age-old foes: these good-for-nothing, well-to-do, effete fucking Poms!' As expected, this drew roars of blood curdling indignation from the mob. Taking up sticks, fence posts, and readily constructed brick bats, the crowd moved out of the tents, setting them alight as they left.

The mutiny had begun.

-23-

Northern France, September 9th, 1917

15:00 hrs

Barrett and Renton sat opposite each other in the latter's office. It had been several hours since the former C.O. had been roughly escorted from the building, under armed guard. Statements had been written from all relevant parties, with the exception of Davenport himself, who was in no fit state to perform such a task. The word from the guardroom was that the major had been, in turn, crying, then screaming, then pummelling the barred door in maniacal rage. This news had initially given Renton a satisfied chuckle, though the more he thought about it, the more his smile had faded.

'He's never going to be sent to the front, is he?' He grumbled. 'He's a sure-fire cert for Craiglockhart.'

Craiglockhart, Barrett recalled, had been a rehabilitation centre for men suffering with mental stress including, ironically in Davenport's case, the earliest acknowledgement and treatment for 'shell shock' – a condition he could certainly never be diagnosed with. Barrett tried to offer consolation.

'Maybe. But the way I see it, he was a threat to your operation, which has now, conveniently, gone away.'

Not that Barrett cared one iota. The threat he had really concerned himself with was homicide – an outcome now highly unlikely - at least from Davenport. Renton pointed his mug towards Barrett.

'*Our* operation, laddie.' He said with a smile. 'Don't forget that.' He glanced towards the window, with a thoughtful expression.

'I'm glad I talked Jones around about you.' He looked back, directly into Barrett's eyes. 'I'll not forget what you did with Davenport, this morning...he would have put one in me, had you not intervened.' Barrett smiled back modestly.

He would have emptied all six chambers if I hadn't intervened...which still begs the question: Why you didn't move, as Davenport took a bead on you?

Instead of asking the question, Barrett merely raised his own tea mug in salutation.

Renton stood, walking over to the large filing cabinet in the corner. He ran his hand over the padlock -- still secured -- and glanced back with a raised eyebrow.

'I was meaning to ask, how the hell did you get those dockets out?'

Before Barrett could answer, there came the sound of heavy footfalls from someone running down the corridor. Both men looked at the door as it swung open to reveal Simmons, heaving with exertion. Some seconds passed as the adjutant struggled to regain sufficient breath to speak. Eventually, the words came.

'Sirs...pardon the intrusion. There's been an incident.' Renton looked across to Barrett, then back to the panting soldier.

'Well...?' Renton said, impatiently.

'A redcap has shot one of the Jock...err, I mean, Scotch infantry. The bloody balloon's gone up...' He anxiously looked past the two seated officers, through the window, as if seeing someone. 'The Aussies and the Scotch have gone on the rampage; they've already set fire to some of the tents...someone said they're heading for the town.'

Simmons had hardly finished his sentence and Renton was on his feet, pulling on his field webbing, a grim expression suddenly clouding his face. He eyed Barrett.

'Find that bloody pansy Sumner...' He paused to check that his revolver was loaded. '...and get your gear. Lobby entrance...two minutes.'

Barrett ran back to his own office, mind racing around what he knew had been coming. He had mulled over several alternative plans in the run up to the mutiny, purposefully not fixating on any one option while this unknown environment unravelled before him. Certainly, his infiltration into the bootleggers had given him a beneficial -- if unforeseen -- avenue, previously denied him. The deserters' caves in the woodland, bordering the beach, would provide a good place to hide out while the worst of the insurrection blew over. But, as yet, he had no firm idea as to exactly how he was going to get Renton out of danger. Barrett knew, from the history records, that there would be fatalities, but these were mostly redcaps and canaries – the main target for the rampaging troops' wrath. That said, he also knew that some officers would be amongst the deaths. He couldn't help that; his only aim was to make sure Renton was not one of them.

In the corridor, Barrett nearly collided with Sumner, exiting his own office. He had heard the commotion and he too had pulled on his webbing, swapping cap for helmet as he stepped through the doorway. He stared at Barrett with the same dark expression that seemed forever painted on his troubled face, but said nothing. Joining Renton out front, the captain was busy organising two platoons of men that had been 'scrambled' to form a defensive militia. Each of them carried their Lee Enfield rifles; each of them looking seriously worried – clearly, they had also heard about the uprising. Spinning on his heel, as the two lieutenants walked out across the veranda, he issued the plan of action.

'The depot's standing orders, in such an unlikely situation as this, is one of lock down containment. B-Company's part of this is control of entry and egress into the town via the only route in our sector, the railway bridge crossing.' Renton jerked a thumb at Sumner.

'Lieutenant Sumner, I want you to take these men and blockade the railway bridge.' He nodded towards a lance corporal standing nearby. 'The word is that there is a mob growing in strength, whose main aim appears to be the looting of the town. It is likely that this will be their path, since this is probably the softest route, avoiding the main gate.' He made no mention of the redcap, or what he had done. Barrett saw Sumner's eyes, widening in horrified panic as Renton went on. 'That mob is *not* to leave camp via that route, am I understood?'

Sumner was shaking his head slowly, in disbelief.

'What are your orders if they don't want to turn around?' He asked quietly, trying to prevent the milling soldiers from hearing him. Renton's dislike for Sumner wasn't really subtle before, now it was positively transparent.

'*Sir.*' Renton interjected waspishly. Sumner made a confused face. Renton continued. 'What are your orders if they don't want to turn around...sir!' He waited petulantly for Sumner to repeat the question, with the added amendment. Only then did Renton answer, his voice dripping venom.

'I would have thought that was obvious lieutenant.' He looked past Sumner's shoulder, raising his voice so that the soldiers could all hear him. 'Do you want me to spell it out?' he shouted. The yelled question had one purpose: to undermine Sumner's standing, in front of the men.

But why?

Sumner swallowed hard, cheeks turning from crimson to deep purple.

'Yes sir. I would like my orders to be clear.'

Renton somehow sneered and tutted simultaneously. In the same loud and obnoxious manner, he replied, though he was really addressing everyone.

'Very well. Lieutenant Sumner: you are ordered to blockade the railway bridge with the task of preventing the crossing of said bridge by mutinous fucking scum. *As mutinous fucking scum, these men are committing treason* and, therefore, should your position be threatened with deadly force, you are hereby authorised to defend yourselves, and the bridge, with the same deadly force.' A murmur rose up from the assembled men, but Renton ignored it. His fiercely burning eyes were fixed on Sumner's. 'In other words, lieutenant...your orders are to shoot them!' He stared into Sumner's eyes. 'Do you accept your orders?' A slight, if wicked, smile played across the captain's lips. Barrett thought for a moment that Renton *wanted* Sumner to say no – another treasonous act, he could then prosecute?

A long moment of silence followed. Out of the corner of Barrett's eye he caught a flicker of movement. Looking down, he could see Sumner's hands, hanging by his sides, shaking, just like he'd seen the night before in the Mess corridor, outside Sumner's room. Eventually, Sumner's quavering voice uttered two words.

'Yes sir.'

As Sumner's detail marched away, Barrett could see Renton dishing out orders and instructions to a few other men, Simmons included. While waiting, he tried to remember the case files he had digested about the beginning of the mutiny. He recalled that the railway bridge route, into town, *had* been of significance. There had been a standoff there, where troops had been positioned to perform the exact task Renton had just specified. Wisely, the officer in charge had not followed his standing order and had allowed the mob through. It was widely recognised that had he not done so, the mutiny would have taken a far more destructive path, rather than, eventually, petering out, as it did. Seeing Sumner's reaction to the order, it was clear that he *was* that rational officer; his higher moral code meant that a bloodbath would be averted; he was precisely the right man, in the right place, at the right time. Even if he looked like he was about to have a nervous breakdown, Barrett pondered grimly. Barrett's attention turned back to Renton. The captain looked irritated.

'Where's that idiot Lyman? Have you seen him?' Renton asked, furtively looking this way and that. Barrett hadn't, but he knew very well why. He offered a likely reason, feigning speculation.

'I've been thinking about that. Simmons said that all this has stemmed from a redcap shooting one of the men. It stands to reason the mob won't take too kindly to redcaps at the moment...or canaries for that matter. If he's got any sense, Lyman is probably laying low for now.'

Barrett was building a case to justify that they should do the same, for the same reasons. He wasn't hopeful that this plan would be enough, however. The idea of hiding from -- to use Renton's own words -- 'mutinous fucking scum' would be fiercely opposed, he was sure. Barrett smirked slightly to himself, momentarily thinking how -- for Renton at least -- the notion of mutiny was so objectionable...while bootlegging was just fine and dandy. Before he could continue his persuading efforts, Renton surprised him.

'You make a good point, laddie.' He looked across at Davenport's staff car, parked in front of the veranda. 'I think we need to get out of the way for a while.'

Barrett followed Renton's gaze.

'Where did you have in mind?' he asked. Renton smiled conspiratorially.

'A place that no-one knows about, of course...the caves.'

Well, that was easy Barrett thought, though he had reservations.

'Not sure about the car though, sir. It's a little bit high profile, don't you think?' He could see immediately that Renton was having none of it.

'Nonsense. Besides, the previous owner won't mind.' He chuckled wryly. 'Anyway, this'll soon blow over.'

Driving through the camp gates, Barrett noticed evidence of the depot ramping up in readiness to meet the growing threat. The guard complement looked to have been tripled, and all were overseen by a brawny sergeant, holding what looked like a large wooden club. Renton had merely to show his face for the car to be let through; even for such a massive camp as Étaples, he was clearly well known – that could prove problematic, Barrett thought. The car rumbled up the dusty road, and after barely a kilometre, Renton swung the steering wheel, careering the vehicle onto a rough track cutting through the skirting woodland, towards the sand dunes. Barrett had not seen the cave, or its approaches, in the daylight. He'd been unconscious on his last visit *into* the hideout, and on foot for his way out of it. The car was following a path of sorts, Barrett noticed, though the undergrowth of the bushes and trees largely masked any obvious route, and the winding, snaking route made Barrett consider how well the terrain had hidden the deserters all this time. Renton glanced sideways at Barrett, misconstruing Barrett's expression.

'Relax about the car, laddie. No-one comes out here, and besides...as you said, everyone's going to be busy enough with what's going on.'

Barrett nodded agreement. It was true enough. Right about now, if he remembered the case notes accurately, many of the officers were being unceremoniously bundled into the back of a motor lorry, after which they would be tipped into the nearby stream cutting through the camp. Whilst a thorough dunking was hugely humiliating, it hadn't developed into anything more serious – for the majority of the 'brass'. He couldn't have attested to this being the only treatment Renton would have received, however. He had clearly played a much more 'hands-on' role than many of the officer cadre, he and his little band of canaries.

As the car negotiated a tight turn around a large sand dune, Barrett was suddenly flung forwards into the large, leather-padded dashboard, as the brakes were violently applied. The car had very nearly tailgated one of three army lorries blocking their path. Renton had inadvertently let the car stall and now he sat, mouth open, staring at several pairs of soldiers, all carrying different boxes and cartons out from the cave mouth, packing them into the trucks.

All the supplies. All the contraband. All the profits.

All *his* profits.

-24-

Northern France, September 9th, 1917

18:30 hrs

Barrett could see an officer advancing towards them, as they sat looking at the logistical effort being made to empty the cave of its ill-gotten gains. Barrett glanced sideways at Renton. The captain was completely immobile, a frozen sitting statue, hands loosely gripping the steering wheel, mouth agape. He poked a finger into the captain's thigh, trying to break his trance.

'Sir?' he said in a hushed but urgent tone. 'Al...?' A little louder.

Nothing. Renton remained transfixed. Simply staring ahead. As the officer drew level with the driver's seat, Barrett could see the one shoulder pip of a second lieutenant.

Well, at least that's something. Barrett thought, with some relief. The young officer brought himself to attention and performed a crisp salute. Renton didn't even look at him. Breaking the awkward silence, Barrett took the initiative.

'Report, lieutenant.' He said simply. The officer, still waiting for acknowledgement of his salute, remained at attention, looking at Renton with uncertainty and some slight consternation. Slowly, he lowered his arm, redirecting his gaze towards Barrett.

'Errr, well...the intelligence we received turned out to be correct, sir.' He nodded back towards the lorries. 'As you can see, they had established quite the goldmine.' He stopped to offer a slight chuckle. 'We may need another lorry, at this rate.' When neither of the two officers reacted to the witticism, he went on. 'We have several men in custody, though I am sorry to report that the leader has eluded us.'

Renton's face remained impassive. More by shock than judgement, he was giving nothing away, Barrett presumed. However, worried that the captain might inadvertently blunder out some ill-chosen words, Barrett continued.

'Who has been identified as the ringleader?' Barrett inquired. The lieutenant's expression changed to one of mild confusion. *Suspicion?*

'I assumed you knew, sir. A Private Stanley Jones, formerly of the Cheshires, I gather.'

As if flipping a switch, Renton finally came back to reality. Removing his cap to run his fingers slowly through his hair, he sighed audibly and looked up into the lieutenant's face for the first time. When he spoke, it was with a peeved air of impatience. The change in demeanour was dramatic and Barrett thought, not for the first time, how it manifested evidence of real pathological instability.

'Of course, we were aware of Jones, lieutenant. My colleague's enquiry is in regard to *his* superior.' The lieutenant began to stutter a reply.

'I...err, well...we were told that...'

Renton interrupted harshly.

'You don't imagine that all of this has been masterminded by a bloody private, do you?' Authority was firmly back in Renton's voice. Before the young officer could answer again, Renton turned to sit sideways in the car seat, looking at the stumbling subaltern, one eyebrow arched, acting out the role of inquisitor.

'I'm beginning to wonder if you've been given the whole story here, lieutenant...who has verified this intelligence? Who is *your* source?'

Bloody hell, that was masterful Barrett mused, with some admiration.

If the lieutenant held any previous reservations regarding the security clearance of the two officers, he quickly shelved them under the category of 'more than my job's worth'.

'The directive came from OIC B-Company's office, sir: Major Davenport...' Renton, once again, interrupted the young man - who was obviously now wishing he was somewhere else.

'I bloody know who he is, laddie...*I'm* B-Company!...why do you think I'm here? There's been some crossed bloody wires with this debacle, and believe you-me, I'll be getting to the bottom of it.' He ranted on, convincingly. The lieutenant remained quiet, waiting for the storm to pass. He had no clue what this captain was going on about, but he wasn't about to enquire further: Renton's rasping barrage brooked no questioning.

At long last, Renton's invective began to subside.

'Right. I'll leave this in your hands, lieutenant. Make sure every last item is catalogued and accounted for.' He started the car's engine, but then looked up at the young man again. 'And, lieutenant? I am sure you will have also received intelligence that this renegade Jones' methods have also included murder?' This information had obviously *not* been shared with the young officer, but he nevertheless nodded agreement to avoid any further tongue lashing. 'As such, you are to take no chances with our men. Your orders are to shoot on sight. To kill.' Renton waited for acknowledgement.

'Yes sir. Understood.'

So much for nobility among thieves. Barrett thought briefly.

A brief nod to the once more offered salute, and the car was reversing back along the sandy track. The vehicle had barely swung around, and Renton was banging the palm of one hand hard against the steering wheel in barely contained fury.

'Fucking damnation!' he cried.

Renton morosely stirred the teaspoon around the cup, the contents of which had been stone cold for at least half an hour. Barrett waited patiently for the now silent Scotsman to come to terms with events. Given the unfolding drama happening at the depot, and the recent disaster at the cave, the two men had driven Davenport's car across the River Canche into Paris Plage, the nearby main town to the west of the camp. For the last two hours they had sat in a cafe, saying very little. Barrett knew that this place would also feel the effect of the mutiny, but not for a day or two yet. Eventually, Renton broke the silence.

'That bastard had the last laugh eh?' Referring to Davenport. 'He didn't waste any time.' He rubbed at his chin. 'I haven't figured out how he knew where the caves were yet, mind you.'
Barrett had been wondering about that too, though he had a more pressing question.

'I presume Jones was the only one who knew your name?' Renton nodded grimly.

'Aye. We maintained a bit of a need-to-know practice, thank God, though any one of those bastards could identify me on a line up, I've no doubt.' He reached into his breast pocket for his cigarette case, for the fifth time in two hours, lit one and inhaled deeply. As the smoke blew out through his nostrils, he went on. 'It stands to reason he's gonna think I've dobbed him in...if they take him, he'll squeal on me in a heartbeat.'

Hence the shoot-to-kill order, Barrett surmised.

Barrett sat back in his chair, fingers absent mindedly drumming the tabletop. Thinking. What next? His one and only goal had been, and still was, Renton's safety. The cave hideout was 'blown', and he also knew that, before long, Étaples town would become very crowded with the spill over of pleasure-seeking mutineers. He was beginning to suspect the camp might be the better refuge. After all, provided Renton didn't take the mob on, he would come through this unscathed. The records, Barrett recalled, showed that after the initial kneejerk rage of the uprising -- the bloodlust to bring the canaries to 'justice' -- the vast majority of troops had settled down. Most just wanted to get into town to enjoy all the freedoms the officers had partaken of, all this time. After some cajoling, Renton accepted Barrett's suggestion to sneak back into camp, keeping a low profile. Surprisingly, he even agreed to Barrett's advice to ditch the car outside the perimeter fence and mask their rank as much as possible under cover of their great coats.

Within half an hour, the two officers were approaching the main gate, although strangely, Barrett noted, there appeared to be no guards present. When they had passed through earlier, there had been at least six, plus the club-carrying sergeant; now the gate stood open for anyone to waltz in, *or out.* Barrett felt the unease in Renton's voice as he spoke.

'Something isn't right here, laddie,' he said forebodingly.

Barrett agreed. Once again, thinking back to the accounts of this first day of insurrection, he remembered that, after the initial stand-off at the bridge, and the, largely light-hearted, dunking of many of the officers into the Canche tributary, the remainder of the day had proceeded without major incident. Other than putting out fires, the camp had maintained a general functionality, with the only glaring difference being the cessation of training.

Looking into the guard post hut, Barrett could see the disarray where tables and chairs had been upturned. There was clear evidence of looting and indiscriminate damage which suggested a frenzied mob, rather than, at worst, a bunch of angry squaddies. The greater concern, however, was to be found in the adjoining room – the armoury. The gun racks were completely empty. The securing chains used to snake through each rifle trigger guard, lay impotent on the floor, where the padlocks had been cut through with bolt croppers. He wondered briefly where the ammunition was stored, all the time knowing that this would have been raided too with an equal degree of zeal. Just then, he heard the muffled cries of Renton calling his name. He'd gone to investigate the adjacent building, a rest area for the guards when not on sentry.

Barrett walked in to find Renton crouched over a body lying on the floor. From the visible rank on his epaulette, they could see that he was, *had been,* a captain. He was dead. His face was alabaster white, but below his chin, and all across the front of his jacket, was the soaked in colour of dark red blood. Renton looked up at Barrett.

'His throat's been cut.' He said, quietly.

The cadaver lay, face up, his eyes fixed open, staring at the ceiling. His boots were slightly splayed, as if sleeping, but he was partially lying on his arms, his hands tucked beneath his buttocks. Barrett rocked the body carefully to one side, finding what he'd expected to see. The captain's hands had been tied.

This had been an execution.

Renton rose to his feet, unfastening the flap of his revolver holster. Barrett stared up at him, shaking his head slowly. This was more than mob rule; this was slaughter. Before he could utter another word, both men heard a noise that made them instantly freeze. It had come from a cupboard in the corner of the room, behind a rough, fabric covered settee. Renton pointed the gun at the corner and pulled back the cocking lever, but Barrett held up a hand.

'Wait.' He said, moving cautiously and silently around the seat.

Nearing the cupboard, Barrett could hear a shallow breathing behind the thin wooden door. He reached for the handle with one hand, holding up the other to Renton, showing first three fingers, followed by two, counting down. Renton took aim as Barrett reached one, quickly yanking the door wide. Curled up in the unfeasibly tiny space, a man sat shivering, a look of abject terror across his face. He didn't cry out. He was beyond that, Barrett thought. The distinct aroma of stale urine struck Barrett's nostrils and he wondered how many hours the man had been cooped up in there. Gently, he whispered.

'It's alright. No one here wishes you harm. Come on...come on out.' An almost imperceptible shake of the head was the answer. Barrett glanced at Renton who theatrically rolled his eyes skyward. He tried again. 'We need to know what has happened here.' Again, the shake of the head. Trying to think of a different strategy, his thoughts were harshly interrupted by Renton, who had clearly lost whatever patience he had left.

'Do you know who I am?' He thundered, causing the cupboard dweller to jump in fright. The man eyed Renton and, remarkably, nodded his head, and uttered in a croaky voice:

'Yessir...'

Renton smiled and lowered his revolver.

'Now laddie, you can stay in there if you really want to, but you'd better start telling us what you know. Savvy?'

Slowly, painstakingly, like some mysterious Indian Fakir, the man began to uncoil the bodily knot he had tied himself into. It was only as his shoulders cleared the cupboard that Barrett could see the yellow fabric flash around his left upper arm. He was a canary. Renton pulled a chair upright for him to sit down, pulling another one opposite for himself. The Scot offered a cigarette from his opened metal case, which the soldier took with both hands, shaking violently. After some two minutes, Renton again addressed him.

'From the top then, son, go on.'

Stood at the doorway, looking out for signs of activity and any possible return of the mob, Barrett heard the canary recount his horrible tale. He told Renton everything he knew. And that was plenty.

After the initial uprising -- a few burning tents and huts -- the main complement of mutineers had, as predicted, tried to head out into Étaples town. They had taken the shortest route which, as assumed, had been via the railway bridge. The mob had found Sumner's blockade waiting for them.

This is where things went wrong.

As Barrett had remembered from the recorded archives, after the initial face off, sense had prevailed and, to avoid inevitable bloodshed, the officer in charge had commanded the barricade to be opened up, letting the mutineers through.

This is not what had happened, however.

Details were sketchy. What *was* clear was the mob had *not been let through*. Instead, they had been engaged with deadly force. Not one or two shots, but a fusillade of *effective* rifle fire. Other than the odd brick bat, the majority of mutineers had been unarmed. Estimates of dead and wounded were as high as thirty. It was carnage between soldiers of the same British army, on an unprecedented scale.

And it wasn't supposed to happen.

As the canary continued to describe the horror, Barrett searched his memory of the incident he had read about. Why had things taken such a terrible turn *against history?* He wished he could remember the details, but he couldn't. What was apparent, however, was that they, he and Renton, as officers, were now, more than ever, in deadly danger. Even worse, as Barrett had just recently witnessed, Renton's face was so recognisable -- so identifiable as *one of them* -- that simply ditching the uniform was not going to be enough. The canary went on to explain that after the bridge massacre, the mob had grown, exponentially. Incensed to a point beyond anarchy, they had marauded back through camp, with intense brutality. To wear a commissioned officer's uniform, a canary arm band or an M.P.'s red cap was to invite death. As far as he'd understood, many of the top brass had been taken out to the Bull Ring. A makeshift scaffold had been erected and several officers had been hung – including Brigadier General Thomas, the camp commandant. The tragedy was complete, *and historically inaccurate.*

Coming to the end of his account, the canary held his head in his hands. His shoulders began to shake, and Barrett realised the man was weeping uncontrollably. In a moment of rare compassion, Renton walked over and rubbed the man's shoulder. As he began to calm himself, Renton whispered something to him, whilst, at the same time, carefully pulling the yellow flash from his arm, throwing it back into the cupboard. The canary rose unsteadily, wiped his dripping nose on a sleeve and quietly walked from the room. Renton watched him go, then slowly, turned back to face Barrett, a set grimness on his face.

'What now?'

-25-

Northern France, September 10th, 1917

02:30 hrs

Barrett threw another pebble at the window. It struck the plate glass with a loud crack, before bouncing off the ledge, and returning to his feet. He was about to give up when the dim light from within the room glared more brightly and he knew he'd managed to wake the occupants. Through the foggy pane, a white face peered out, regarding him for a moment, standing in the alleyway below. The window opened slightly with a rusty creak, and a subdued female voice meekly enquired.

'Who's there?'

Barrett replied at an equally quiet volume.

'I need to see Simone…is she there?'

The face scrutinised the standing man -- probably wondering what on earth he was doing there at such an un-Godly hour -- before disappearing, leaving the window ajar. Barrett waited, and as the seconds turned to minutes, he wondered if anyone was coming back. He felt dangerously exposed, stood, as he was, in the back street behind Le Jardin d'Eden bordello. Even at this time, the main streets were still jumping with cavorting soldiers, most of whom were too drunk to properly walk, let alone be out hunting down camp officials. Nevertheless, he and Renton had kept to the shadows. They had managed to successfully re-clothe themselves, courtesy of several washing lines, between the camp and Étaples town, and now resembled -- at a glance, anyway -- simple peasant folk.

The journey from the main camp gates had been fraught with near misses, as gangs of soldiers, mainly Australians and Scots, had, at times, come to within mere centimetres of them. They had been forced to cower in fields, in bushes, and, on one occasion, had to lay down in a peat bog, their faces pressed into the muddy water. It was during this latest close call that Barrett had deliberated, once again, how events had led to where they were now. His mind had replayed the words of the Horizon executive, Anders, and the government official, Pilgrim, telling him how the 'spatial ripple' had changed things; how Renton's death -- which was never supposed to have happened -- had upset the balance of 'time'. It occurred to him that this new history, unfolding before him, was likely to be the cause. Certainly, by far the most plausible reason for Renton's 'murder', at this present moment, was through some kind of execution-style retribution at the hands of the Étaples mutineers. Yet he still struggled to piece together why everything had skewed so very badly. *So much for the umbrella theory.* Barrett had thought, as he lay blowing bubbles in the mud.

At long last, another face appeared at the open window. It was Simone.

'Who is that? What do you want?' The voice called. Very quietly, Barrett replied back to her.

'My name is Liam. Do you remember me? I saw you two night ago.'

Was it only two nights? It felt like an eternity of time had passed.

The girl didn't react; he never really expected her to. Their one and only meeting had lasted barely an hour. Him sitting in her bedroom, drinking wine. Talking. Realistically, he knew it had been a desperate idea, reaching out to her, but he genuinely didn't know what else to do. Their options had run out. There was likely to be nowhere on camp that hadn't been ransacked or remained extremely unsafe for any member of training or police staff. Similarly, the town itself was extremely hazardous, alive as it was with singing, dancing and, at times, looting, troops.

Some cafes, Barrett had seen, had been hotspots of lively, raucous merry making, with waiters furnishing the soldiers with bottle after bottle of wine, beer and spirits. Other establishments, for some unknown reason, had been completely gutted, their tables and chairs thrown into the centre fountains, their canopies set alight and their windows smashed, the glass decorating the cobbled streets in a twinkling array of light.
Simone stared down for several seconds. It would have been so easy for her to simply pull the window closed again. Instead she replied.

'Wait there.'

Five minutes later the door below the window opened, and Simone came out into the cold morning air, wrapped in multiple layers of clothing. She quietly closed the door behind her and motioned Barrett to follow her down the lane. As they set off, Renton rose from behind the bush where he had been hiding, giving Simone a scare. Upon recognising the captain, she turned on Barrett, her eyes flashing with anger.

'What is the meaning of this? I agree to help you...' She pointed a gloved hand at Renton. '...not him!' She cried, in hushed outrage. Moving close, Barrett reached out his hands to take hold of her shoulders, but she shied away, petulantly.

'Simone, I'm sorry, but you must understand, we are both in very grave danger...' Barrett said imploringly. He guessed she'd already seen the results of this, from the discretionary manner she had displayed so far; however, she had stopped walking, and Barrett felt sure she was about to turn around and go back, unless he could persuade her otherwise.

'Please Simone, if we can't find somewhere to hide...we're dead men.' She stared at Renton with a look of loathing. The hatred in her eyes conveyed that she would be more than happy to see the captain hanging by his neck. Barrett glanced nervously up and down the lane. Despite the early hour, they were in the open, visible, unprotected. They had to get to cover. He tried one more time. 'Simone, I know you have no reason to get involved...' He reached out and held her hands, making her look into his eyes. '...but you've seen what is happening...you know how this will go, if you don't help us...if you don't help *me*.' She squeezed his fingers and, after perhaps ten drawn-out seconds, gave the smallest nod of her head. She spoke softly:

'For you? Oui...' Still holding Barrett's hands, she briefly turned her head towards Renton. '...you? You can go to hell!'

Renton had the good sense to remain quiet and merely followed along sheepishly as the woman began to lead Barrett once more along the alleyway. After several minutes, they had reached the edge of town; walking down a leafy avenue, they came to a large, derelict-looking barn. Simone led the men down the side to an alcove covered entry, producing a key from beneath the folds of her clothes. Unlocking the door, they passed inside. Barrett was immediately struck by how surprisingly warm it was, but as Simone lit a hanging gas lamp, he saw the reason why. From floor to ceiling, bales of hay were stacked in all directions, freshly reaped from the late August-September harvest. Simone nodded up to the dovecot, accessed via a fixed wooden ladder.

'You will be warm and safe here.' She glanced again at Renton with a sneer. 'Alas, there are a lot of *rats* in here too.' Barrett cradled her face with the palms of his hands, staring deep into her eyes.

'Thank you.' He said simply. He knew she was taking a terrible risk harbouring them, especially someone as notorious as Renton. Her sensuous eyes looked back into his. He wanted so much to kiss her. To hold her.

More than that.

A small, interrupting cough detonated through the moment, and Barrett wanted to turn around and shoot the man himself. Instead, Simone pulled away, sensing his frustration. She started to walk back towards the door. Over her shoulder she said:

'I shall lock the door. It will be safer for you this way. I will bring food and drink when I can.'

She didn't look back.

Barrett awoke suddenly with a start, his heart racing out of his chest. Around him, the same still, pitch darkness. Yet something had disturbed him. He cursed whatever had roused him, conscious of his exhaustion. Despite his fatigue, it had taken him long enough to doze off. For the first hour in the barn, he'd struggled to acclimatise to all the noises of the environment: the wind whistling through the rafters; the scurrying of rats coming and going, and the eventual fading sound of men, finally giving up their festivities to crash somewhere -- anywhere -- to sleep off the alcohol. Renton's snoring hadn't helped either. Eventually, weariness had won the fight and he'd slept. Fitfully.

He looked at his watch in the gloom and could just make out the time, a little after 5 a.m. Another hour or so until sunup, he reckoned. If they had anywhere to go, now would have been the ideal time. They didn't. There was one strategy only. To sit and wait. Barrett's mission briefing had estimated a timeframe that was due to expire around the fifteenth – another five days away yet, he thought miserably.

I'm not sure I can handle that...But will I have to?

The original prediction had been made based on the *known* historical sequence of events. In other words, the original timeline.

Where the mutineers' railway bridge crossing hadn't ended in a fucking bloodbath!

Much of the analysis of the mutiny had suggested that the uprising had only lasted as long as it had due to the relatively low-key train of events. Whilst there had been deaths during the original mutiny, there had been nowhere near the scale of carnage experienced over this last twenty-four hours. Ultimately, he pondered, this version should receive a much swifter engagement from the upper chain of command - especially once news of the Brigadier's execution reached them. Retribution would be swift, and it would be brutal.

Barrett looked across at Renton, who was still snoring loudly, adding to the ambient soundtrack of the barn. For perhaps the hundredth time he wondered how this man's life had such an impact, on such an Earth-affecting scale.

No, not Earth-affecting...

...Humanity-affecting.

What was it Jonas Salk had famously said? If all insects died, within fifty years all life on Earth would end. If all humans disappeared, within fifty years, all life would flourish.

He reached down to rub his buttocks; they had become numb sleeping half upright against a massive wall of straw. He started to manoeuvre his body into a more comfortable position when he heard the creak of a floorboard. He froze.

Was that the sound that had woken me?

Listening intently, he waited to hear the sound repeat, but there was only silence. Even so, the hairs on the back of his neck stood up with the age-old, uncanny recognition of danger. Sitting perfectly still, his eyes scanned around for his revolver. Swearing inwardly, he remembered that he'd removed it from his coat pocket to use the garment as a makeshift pillow. He knew the gun was sat on a small bale some two metres away. He stared into the dark from where the noise had come from, trying to somehow triangulate its origin. He was sure it had been from somewhere below them, down the ladder, underneath the dovecot. Barrett eased himself over onto his side so he could reach out for the gun. In the gloom, he made out the black straight line of the floor start to change as a small, dark shape began to rise up out of it, with infinite slowness. With growing dread, he realised it was a head, coming up through the hatch. Barrett froze again, fearful that any more movement would betray his position and, for a fleeting instant, he imagined getting to the gun, only to shoot Simone, trying her hardest not to disturb their rest.

No...it wasn't Simone.

But, whoever this was, they knew that the two men were there. There was no other explanation for the stealthy entrance. And, this being so, Barrett thought, the certainty was that they meant them no good. Deciding to make a quick reach for the revolver, he was suddenly blinded by the stark wash of torchlight, hitting him straight in the eyes, accompanied by an oddly familiar voice.

'Move and you're dead.'

-26-

Northern France, September 10th, 1917

05:15 hrs

'Slowly, light the oil lantern next to you.' The voice was harsh, business like. Not to be taken lightly. Barrett picked up the matchbook lying next to the lamp and lit the wick. He was still bathed in the yellow torch beam that, in the pitch-dark barn, seemed to shine like a lighthouse. Blowing the match out, the lamplight brightened the space significantly, but the interloper remained in relative darkness, hidden behind the torch beam. Barrett chanced a glance toward the bearer.

'Can you kill the light? I can't see a bloody thing.' He asked. The stranger chuckled a little.

'That's the point, chum, but you ought to shut it or I'll be killing something else.' The torch beam remained. 'Wake that bastard up; he'd sleep through a fuckin' earthquake.' Barrett made to move. 'Carefully...I can see your gun, but I can't see his...either way, if you move in a way I don't like, it's all over for you.'

Slowly and deliberately, Barrett poked the toe of his right boot into Renton's ribs. This needed a few attempts; the stranger had been right, the big captain wasn't easy to rouse. After one more determined jab, Renton lifted his head up, dazedly looking first towards Barrett, then into the light, raising a hand to mask his eyes. The voice seemed delighted.

'There he is. Nice to see you, Al, my old mate.' At this, Barrett recognised the voice.

This wasn't good. He understated to himself.

Renton rubbed at his eyes, slowly coming back to consciousness. He didn't sound concerned when he addressed Private Jones, ex-partner-in-crime.

'You've always been a slippery customer, Stan. Always one step ahead of them eh?' Renton said, in a sleepy, conversational tone. Jones, whether annoyed by the flippancy of Renton's remark, or the nonchalance of his manner, retorted harshly.

'No thanks to you, you backstabbing bastard.' He had pulled himself fully into the dovecot now, the torch beam wavering a little as he did so. 'Sold the bloody lot of us down the river...after all we'd achieved...' His voice had taken on an emotional quaver. 'Oh yes, you did a number on us, Captain Renton, sir...your team scooped the whole gang...well, nearly...' He paused, sniffing; Barrett assumed he was wiping his nose, though he still couldn't see Jones, past the bright light. '...you'd 'ave got me too, if I hadn't needed to go for a shit.' He chuckled at this, though there was little humour in the sound. 'Funny how fate works eh? I've been thinking about that ever since.'

'Oh yeah?' Renton replied, going along with the dialogue as if patiently humouring on a child. Barrett cringed at this attitude, and for a brief moment, he remembered how Renton had passively awaited inevitable death in Davenport's office, the day before.

Was he suicidal?

Jones, went on, oblivious to Renton's condescension.

'Yeah. You see I've never been much of a believer...but *something* made me leave that cave, so that I didn't get nabbed with everyone else...'

Renton yawned with the over accentuated sound of boredom. Unsurprisingly, this was not lost on Jones.

'You fucking bastard...' The torch beam was shaking now, with rage. '...you needn't worry about yawning; you'll be sleeping soon enough.' A long silence passed, as Jones tried to regain his composure. Barrett was bewildered at Renton's apparent indifference in the face of death. There was no tactic he could imagine that would give them the advantage by making Jones even angrier than he already was. The ex-private had them zeroed. He couldn't miss at such close range and pissing him off would only bring the end sooner. Eventually, Jones continued, determined to share his epiphany.

'So...as I was saying: Something made me go to answer Nature's call. And I'm thinking: "Why did that happen?" Like I said, I've been giving that a lot of thought, and do you know what I came up with?' He paused, despite the rhetorical question, as if waiting for an answer. 'I was spared for one reason...to send you to hell.'

The double click of the cocking lever of the Webley was unmistakable in the darkness. Barrett assumed Renton would be first, silently gauging if he could make it to his own pistol in time to return fire. Hardly. Even if he managed it, he would still be firing wildly, semi-blinded by the torch. Renton, at last, piped up.

'Stan, you've never been a fool; don't start now. I didn't dob you in. What would be the gain in that? I've lost everything, same as you...why would I do it?' His voice remained calm, his questions logical. He still wasn't a man begging for his life, and, Barrett thought, never would be. Despite the cocked weapon, Jones was prepared to discuss; clearly, he was in no rush.

'Self-preservation.' Jones replied. 'You'd been rumbled; your way out was to let us all swing, so as to save your own skin.'

Renton shook his head.

'That doesn't make any sense, Stan. Do you think I'd be able to bargain my way out of something like this, just by offering up the boys? How would I explain how I knew where the cave was, and hope to get away with it? They'd have had me in shackles by now. I'm telling you...I didn't dob you in!' There was still no implored whimpering from Renton. Though, Barrett noted, what *did* seem of importance to the Scotsman, was the imperative of not being thought of as a traitor. Renton went on. 'I still don't know how he knew, but it was Davenport who sent in the troops. He'd been after me for a long while; I can only assume that he suspected something and had me followed.' Renton slumped back against the straw wall behind him. 'Look, I don't give two shits whether you believe me or not. I've told you the truth, that's it.'

Another long moment passed, and Barrett fleetingly wondered whether Renton had got through to the would-be executioner. His explanation sounded plausible because it was all true. Exactly how Davenport had homed in on the bootleggers, they would never know; but the rest of it made sense. There was only one crucial problem. Jones chuckled again, this time with a little more mirth.

'Bravo, Al; that was a good attempt, I'll give you that. I would applaud, but my hands are full.'

Renton shrugged his shoulders and opened his hands, palms uppermost as if to question why he had not been believed. Jones delivered the coup de grace.

'All of what you've said is possible. It's also possible that your newfound friend is the cause...' Barrett imagined the gun pointing towards him. '...some things we'll never know, I suppose; but let me tell you something I do know for sure. A little bird told me that you'd issued a shoot-on-sight order for me. Now...' he paused menacingly. '...let me hear you fucking deny that one.'

Renton's hands dropped into his lap. A thin smile of resignation crept across his face. He said no more. After a few moments, Jones spoke again.

'Right. This is it. Make your peace.'

Renton held up one hand, then motioned to one of his breast pockets. Jones, slightly impatiently, replied to the implied gesture.

'Alright. But be quick.' Renton pulled his cigarette case from his pocket and, using the same matchbook as Barrett had used to light the oil lantern, sparked up for his last smoke. Barrett found the exhaled fumes strangely calming, despite having never smoked in his life. One thing intrigued him, and he used the temporary reprieve to ask about it.

'How did you know we were here, by the way?' This brought another chuckle from Jones. He was happy to answer.

'Well now, for that you can also blame our traitorous captain, here. You see your little girlfriend made the mistake of telling Madame Dominque that she'd helped the two of you. Only trouble was, the good Madame was none too fond of old lover boy here...'
Barrett's mind raced back to the night in the bordello; the fleeing prostitute from Renton's room; the blazing row with Dominique in the aftermath. '...turns out his kinks were too much, even for the Garden to put up with. And so, imagine my surprise when Dominque drops your whereabouts into my lap. I'd been laying low in the good lady's care, you see, so when this glorious news was delivered...well...let's just say your situation suited both our needs.'

Renton, down to the last few drags of his cigarette, pinched the end between thumb, and forefinger and flicked it away. Slowly, he raised himself from the floor, so as to stand up to accept his sentence, pulling his jacket down to straighten out the creases. Staring into the torch beam, unrepentant, he awaited his end.

The shot rang out in a deafening cacophony.

-27-

Northern France, September 10th, 1917

06:00 hrs.

The torch flashed briefly skyward, then hit the floor with enough force to extinguish it. It was quickly followed by the potato sack *crump* of Jones' body, falling forwards. Now emerged from behind the shroud of the torch beam, Barrett saw Private Jones for the first time, since the cave. The private's self-incarceration at Le Jardin d'Eden appeared to have done him few favours. His clothes were similar to the ones they wore -- typical peasant garb -- but his were filthy and torn, attesting, no doubt, to the ditches he'd navigated, and the wire fences he's scaled, in his evasion of searching military police. It took both Barrett and Renton a few seconds more to appreciate what had happened. The latter had even patted the front of his torso, seemingly confused as to why he couldn't feel the pain from the fired shot. Only when they stared at Jones' dead body did realisation set in. The entry wound couldn't be seen amid the matted quagmire of Jones' muddy tunic, but it was obvious the shot had taken him in the back. Possible from only one direction. Still staring, rooted to the spot, both men saw first the revolver, then the khaki wearing arm, and, finally, the shoulders and head of their saviour emerging through the dovecot hatch.

Lieutenant Sumner.

Were it not for the shock, Barrett could have cried with elation. In that moment, his sole emotion was sheer joy. After days of anguish, tragedy and a stultifying lack of quality sleep, he wanted to run across the dovecot and hug the man who had turned up, in the nick of time. Such was his jubilation, he did not pause to wonder how the young lieutenant had found them; how, at such an early hour, Sumner had *happened* to be in this part of the town, when all around was such mayhem, especially for commissioned officers...wearing uniform, no less. In fact, the only thought, having any success in penetrating the triumph was:

Why was he still pointing his gun towards us?

Sumner had completed his climb up the ladder and was now standing level with the two ex-prisoners. Only, it didn't seem as though they were ex-prisoners...Barrett considered, *not yet*. Neither Renton, nor Barrett said anything at first, but both knew something wasn't right. Much like Jones, Sumner's appearance was very unkempt. His hair was dirty and tousled; his boots, puttees and knees were caked in mud and the stitching, joining his right arm to the shoulder of his jacket, was pulled, giving Barrett the inappropriately comic image of a poorly cared for teddy bear. Only then did Barrett remember what the young officer had been through. He recalled the shaking canary from the main gate house describing the massacre at the railway bridge. For a brief moment, he imagined the young lieutenant yelling commands above the screaming carnage as volley after volley cut the mutineers down, 0.303 calibre ammunition, scything through the bodies. At last, Sumner spoke, with quiet purpose.

'Sit down, both of you.'

Silence for a moment. Trying to comprehend. Then, Renton came alive. Despite being saved from certain death, mere minutes before, the captain regained his voice *and* his authority, applying both towards Sumner in his usual brusqueness.

'Sit down? I think not lieutenant. What we need to do...'

For the second time that morning, the ear-splitting din of a revolver, fired at close range, filled the room. In a microsecond, Barrett saw the last few days dissolve before his eyes. The mission was for naught. The preparation, the complexity, the technological invention of it all...all dust.

Tearing his eyes away from the gaping chasm of the revolver barrel, which was now pointing at him, he looked down at where Renton had dropped. In the dim half-light, cast by the oil lantern, he could see the big man splayed out on the floor. The blood pumped from his thigh, where the bullet had lanced through the quadricep muscle, in a worryingly rapid, pulse flow. Renton was unconscious. He may already be dead, Barrett considered, in that brief instant. That was the one thing the movies always got wrong. The hero could always grit his or her teeth, even after multiple hits in the arms or legs. 'It's just a flesh wound' they would always say, adding to the cliché. Barrett knew better. The combined devastation of a high impact round, tearing through muscle, bone and blood vessels, alongside the hidden menace, shock, where the sudden flood of adrenaline into the blood stream had often dealt the victim a perfect storm that the heart just couldn't recover from. He looked back at Sumner, raising his hands in the age-old tradition. He felt sure that if he had wanted to kill the captain, he would have placed the round elsewhere. But that was an assumption too far at this point.

'Sit...down.' Sumner repeated, equally as composed as he had been before. As Barrett slowly lowered himself to the ground, folding his legs beneath him, he noticed Sumner's hand, holding the pistol. Unlike the earlier occasions recently, it wasn't shaking. Maintaining his aim, Sumner walked slowly over to a square bale of hay, seating himself on top. He motioned with the gun towards Barrett's coat.

'Tear off a piece of that to stem the flow. I don't want him shuffling off, just yet.' As Barrett reached for the coat, Sumner added: 'But be careful, Liam. I think I have suitably shown my resolve.'

Barrett struggled at first to make anything that would act as a bandage. He really could have done with a knife, but Sumner's eyes dissuaded him from asking. Using his teeth, he tore at the hem of the coat, eventually pulling out some reasonably even strips. Working steadily, he tied the coat around the wound, using three strips of the cloth to pull it all tightly together. It was difficult going. The blood was extremely sticky, and he could taste the iron in his mouth as he fought to get the damage under control. The good news, he noted with relief, was that the *flow* had eased to an *ooze*. He was fairly certain the round had missed the main artery, but Renton's face had already gone a deathly grey colour, which didn't bode well.

Satisfied he had done as much as he could, Barrett slumped back against the straw, panting with exertion. The last few days had highlighted his inadequacies at first aid. The days of applying direct pressure were long gone in the midst of laser cauterisers and instant graft patches. Of course, as a police investigator, he had to know how to do things 'the old-fashioned way', but he'd never really performed any of it in anger. He reached out a hand to feel Renton's neck, searching for the carotid artery. The pulse was slow and weak. He grimaced.

'If we don't get him to the hospital, I'm not sure he's going to make it.' Barrett said, eyeing Sumner grimly. Sumner shrugged slightly, the gun resting on his knee, but still pointing directly at Barrett.

'I don't think you're quite seeing the picture here, Liam. I don't want him to make it.'

Barrett searched the lieutenant's face. The young man's expression was calm and collected, yet it was obvious that, for the second time in just an hour, vengeance appeared to be on the agenda. He tried to wipe the viscous blood from his hands, using the material of his trousers, at the same time contemplating his mission, once more. Nothing had gone well. Nothing. The sheer quantity of factors that had stacked up against him was bordering on farcical, he mused, fighting the urge to smile with self-pity. To send him back into the past, to prevent a man's death -- aside from the technical miracle that had enabled the journey in the first place -- the task was almost guaranteed to fail from the outset. Keeping the man safe during one of the bloodiest periods of history had already been nigh-on impossible, but since arriving here, the addition of so many would-be murderers, had all dutifully lined up, like suspects in a game of Cluedo: Davenport, Dominique, Jones, and now, Sumner.

Agatha Christie would have found it all rather ridiculous. He thought despairingly.

Yet, as nonsensical as it was, Barrett was still an investigator, and a damn fine one. Yes, Renton was in a bad way, but he had to believe there was still a way out. He had to engage the young lieutenant, seek out the angles. He tried to think back to his negotiator training days. What had they always impressed on him? Try to work towards their agenda. Try to establish what they want.

'It's maybe a little premature, Lionel, but I guess I should thank you. I don't know what your plans are for me, but...' he nodded towards the dead body of Jones. '...I know what *he* had in mind.'

Sumner smiled thinly, brushing his hair back with his other hand. He sighed dejectedly.

'My plans, as you call them, have become quite a bit more complicated, over the last few days.' He paused to stare at the immobile Renton, his eyes boring into him. 'Ever since I got here, that pig has been successful in fucking my head up.'

Ignoring the odd turn of phrase, Barrett sought to empathise; what had they said? *Try to maintain an accord. Try to find common ground.*

'He's an odd fish, you're right about that. I've been trying to figure out what has been his beef with you...' He paused to temporarily gauge how his words were being received. Sumner simply looked back at him, a very slight curl of a smile, forming on his lips.

'And what have you figured out, Holmes?' He asked sarcastically.

Barrett knew it would be folly to point out the repercussions of shooting an officer. If they made it through this, there would be a far larger inquest for the gunning down of the mutineers, even if he could prove that he was carrying out a direct order. No. The lieutenant was way past all of this. The fundamental matter at hand was Renton. How had he driven Sumner to the point of committing murder? If he could draw this out, like poison from a snake bite, perhaps the act of catharsis might make Sumner think twice. And maybe they could get out of this, alive. He tried his best.

'Well...it seemed to me that things started to go wrong when he gave you that...special duty...you never told me what that was...' Barrett said. Sumner gave a slight nod. He looked back again at the unconscious Renton, then back at Barrett. He replied.

'OK, we have a little time, I suppose. I didn't want to have to repeat myself; I wanted *him* to hear all this, before I...well...you know.' He tilted the revolver slightly to indicate his unspoken intention. Looking back at Barrett, he gave him a more friendly smile. 'Lord knows, you have a right to hear it.' He glanced at his watch, then at the wall where the beginnings of daylight tried its best to peep through the cracks in the wooden slats. 'How long do you think he has before he bleeds out?' He asked. Barrett looked back at the slowly saturating coat. *Not long*. He thought.

'Two hours...maybe three.' Sumner seemed satisfied with this.

'Very well.' He said, at last. Then began to tell it all.

-28-

Northern France, September 10th, 1917

07:20 hrs.

'You'll recall our wonderful visit to the bordello, some nights past?' Sumner asked, hitching himself back on the hay bale, trying to find comfort. Barrett nodded. 'Well, that was the start of it, as far as this bastard was concerned.' Barrett raised an eyebrow, causing Sumner to chuckle.

'Come on, Holmes...piece it together. Do you remember me not being too enamoured with the visit?'

'Well, yes. But neither of us were exactly happy about it.' Barrett replied, remembering his own comments to the young man, in the back seat of the car.

'No one can make you do anything you don't want to, Lionel.'

'Well, what neither you, nor anyone could have known, was that it *really* wasn't for me...if you follow my meaning.' Sumner said, leaving the statement hanging in the air, waiting for Barrett to form the conclusion. Searching his memory, Barrett replayed event.

He'd been nervous...
...no wedding band...
...a virgin?

229

He remembered Renton's lascivious introduction; the Madame...mentioning Barrett's sad eyes. What was it that she'd said to Sumner? He glanced up at Sumner, who seemed to be enjoying Barrett's frustration.

She'd started to say something, but he'd interrupted her...in French! Of course, he had no idea what was said. But...there was something else...before that.

Damn it, what did you see Barrett?

When she first spoke to him...she'd *seen* something. *Known* something.

The penny dropped with the thud of a lump hammer. He looked up at Sumner, who smiled back, realising he'd figured it out.

'You're gay, aren't you?' Barrett asked. 'Madame Dominique...she knew,...she...'

Sumner broke into laughter.

'Yes, bravo Holmes. She *did* know! I'll admit, I don't quite know *how* she knew. I appreciate it's not for everyone.' He chuckled warmly. 'I suppose, in her profession, she gets to see all types. Quite the remarkable deduction though, I thought.' Before Barrett could ask more, Sumner continued. 'I guess this 'finding' was passed on during Dominique's argument with our captain here...' He had stopped laughing now, his face returning to solemnity as he imagined Renton seething over the knowledge that one of his officers was *one of them*.

'Certainly, after that, he had my card marked.' He sneered at the body laid out on the floor. 'The fucking hypocrisy...the irony! His sexual proclivities extend to rape, though he fucking loathes me for what he thinks is...unnatural. Fucking homophobic dinosaur!' And with that, he spat a small wad of phlegm at the prone Captain.

Homophobic...?

Sumner continued.

'So, yes, that was the start of it...but, by Christ, it wasn't the end of it. As you said, the special duty was an important factor. You see, I could deal with the absurdity of homophobia...'

That phrase again...

'...but, sending me out with that little psychopath, Lyman, was something I had not been prepared for, even with all my training.'

This was the crux of it now, Barrett was certain. Sumner had lost his calmness suddenly. He was visibly stressed. The small, tell-tale signs began to show. Rapid swallowing...gulping down air, clearing his throat, in-between words. He had paused for a moment, as if searching for the right things to say. Pulling out a dirty handkerchief, he dabbed at his eyes, then rubbed his nose with it. Looking back at Barrett, he confessed.

'A firing squad, Liam. That was the 'special duty'. No explanation, you will remember...not from him, not even from fucking Lyman, until he'd driven me out there. They were waiting for me, you see...to issue the command. Apparently, it had to be an officer...' His eyes had become red rimmed, near tears, and not for the first time, Barrett considered. Sumner went on. 'The prisoners were supposedly deserters...or had run away during the action.' He coughed several times, his voice quivering. 'Most were no older than teenagers, Liam; they were petrified...someone had pinned a white piece of paper over their hearts...something to aim for...' He broke off, words catching in his throat. The revolver bounced in his hand, and Barrett wondered, for a fleeting moment, if he could have made a dive for it. He decided against it. 'So, I had to give the order. Me.' He looked deep into Barrett's eyes, as if searching for some forgiveness. 'Nothing had prepared me...there was nothing in the training for this...' He broke down. The tears streaming down his face, cutting clean tracks across his dirty cheeks. Barrett started to slowly get up; he genuinely felt for the man, wanted to console him.

The gun came up quickly, once again, pointing at his chest. Sumner, amidst the tears, shook his head. He wasn't finished. Not yet.

'Well...that wasn't the worst of it.' He wiped his sleeve across his face. 'Turned out that most of the firing squad were drunk...three sheets to the wind...I couldn't blame them. I'd been hoodwinked into this misery, but they'd been ordered to do it, based on their skill as sharp shooters. Well, you can probably imagine how accurate they were in that state...' Another pause, another large swallow of air. '...from a line-up of six prisoners, not a single one was killed outright...'

Oh My God

'...some had even been shot more than once...' Barrett thought Sumner was about to flood again, but instead, he sighed, disconsolately staring into the distance, as he recalled the prisoners' agonising, slow deaths. 'Apparently, the duty of the OIC -- should this unfortunate mishap arise -- is to finish them off with the old Webley.' He shook the revolver pseudo-playfully at Barrett. 'That fucker, Lyman was shouting in my ear...telling me I had to do it, that it was up to me to end their suffering...' He jumped down off the bale and planted several rage-filled kicks into Renton's ribcage.

'...THEIR SUFFERING!' He shouted, incensed.

Barrett could do nothing. He sat there, impotently, as Sumner booted the unconscious captain, the body just moving slightly from the impacts. He stopped, and simply stood there, looking down at the immobile sack at his feet. For three long minutes, Sumner let the anger pour out of him in uncontrollable sobbing, the revolver hanging loosely by his side, his finger still curled dangerously around the trigger.

Barrett glanced surreptitiously at his watch. It was nearly 8 a.m. A little over an hour since Renton had been shot. It was difficult to gauge, but the makeshift dressing was now entirely saturated. The original estimate of blood loss was definitely over ambitious, he pondered. Conservatively, he reckoned the captain had an hour, no more. Sumner was just climbing back up into the dovecot, having collected his canteen of water from where he'd left his webbing and great coat, below. Before going, he'd gathered their revolvers, along with a superfluous warning against heroics. This had left Barrett precious little time to reconnoitre the loft space for options, for any advantage he could use. There was nothing up there, he realised sombrely: just bales of hay, a rapidly dying man, and...one other item: perhaps, his last resort.

After Sumner's catharsis, Barrett had stayed quiet for a while. The rest of the story appeared to be straightforward. He knew, after all, that Renton had sent Sumner off to command the detail charged with securing the railway bridge, the following day. As damaged as Sumner obviously was, Barrett could easily piece together the unfolding tragedy. A man, driven to the edge by the cruelty of a sociopathic basket case like Renton, then put in charge of a group of armed soldiers, already pent up with extreme stress. As he'd already been forced to issue a fire order against bound, gagged and defenceless men, it wasn't beyond the realms of possibility that he could repeat the command against a mob of dangerous mutineers. The obvious fact was simple: Sumner was suffering from PTSD, perhaps the worst case of it he'd ever seen.

He glanced again at Sumner. The lieutenant was peering out through the wall slats. Barrett couldn't see what he was looking at, but he could hear the town waking up. The odd vehicle passing down the main street. The sound of glass being swept up and deposited in bins – perhaps in readiness for the next round of revelry, later. Sumner looked down at Renton's still motionless form, then back at Barrett.

'The bastard isn't going to grace us with his presence, is he?' His question contained a mixture of disgust and disappointment. Barrett shook his head slowly. If he couldn't get Renton to medical care, and specifically, a substantial blood transfusion, soon, it would be all over. He had to act. He had one idea remaining, and it was a pretty pathetic one, he admitted to himself.

'Looks like you're going to get your revenge, Lionel. But, I'm guessing, not exactly how you'd preferred it.' Barrett said. Sumner scoffed.

'Dead is dead, Holmes. True enough, I did want him to hear what I had to say...but it would have made no difference. Not to a bastard like him. My only recompense is that his end will mean that no one else has to receive his particular brand of poison.'

Barrett knew it had to be now. He began to put his meagre plan into action. He spoke up.

235

'Would you stop calling me that? Apart from being a figment of someone's imagination, Sherlock Holmes, was a great detective...I, on the other hand, couldn't even see the pain he was causing you...' He said, pseudo-sympathetically. He made an act of being in pain himself, gripping his leg overtly. 'May I stand? My legs have gone to sleep.' Sumner looked at him suspiciously for a moment, but then agreed.

'Fine, but remember...' Waving the revolver, the message was clear. Barrett made a show of slowly getting to his feet. He turned his back towards Sumner, rubbing his hands over his backside and hamstrings, emphasising relief. At the same time, he slowly positioned his body in between the lieutenant and the oil lantern. Sumner, oblivious to this, continued on, good-naturedly.

'I'm sorry Liam, but...my understanding was that you *were* a detective...and a very good one.' Barrett stepped closer to the lantern; it would take half a second to grasp it, another half to spin around and hurl it at Sumner's feet. He estimated the dry hay would catch instantly, giving at least a flash of fire that may be enough to put the man off balance, then he could...

What did he just say?

The blood in Barrett's veins froze.

Barrett slowly turned around, the lantern forgotten. After several pregnant seconds, he asked.

'What do you mean?'

Sumner offered a weak smile but said nothing. Barrett felt a queasiness in his stomach, exactly like the experience he'd had on his arrival, back in the field, outside camp. He felt sure, like that first time, he was about to throw up. He lamely pointed to the water canteen.

'Would you mind if I...?' Sumner nodded, passing the bottle to him. As Barrett took a swig, his mind raced around a hundred possibilities. Trying to reach a conclusion. Was he referring to the bootlegging operation? To Barrett's late-evening espionage of Renton's office? If so, how did he know? For the first time since Sumner had appeared, Barrett questioned himself over how the young man had known they were even here, in this barn. He'd been so focused on the immediate danger, of Renton bleeding to death, of the mission -- and therefore, the fate of humankind -- dying with him, that he had not even considered just how very convenient it had been that Sumner had arrived, just in time to shoot Jones.

Am I under surveillance?

As if in answer to his thoughts, Sumner motioned for him to sit down again, before chuckling quietly.

'I'm sorry, Liam.' He glanced at his watch again, as if checking to see if he had enough time for what he was about to say. Seemingly satisfied, he went on.

'You had a job to do. So did I. But, neither of us should be here. The experiment didn't play out as it should have.'

No...no...it can't be...

237

'You have done as well as anyone could have hoped; but...ultimately...it's a lost cause, Liam. You can see that can't you?' Sumner said, a tone of disappointed regret in his voice. 'If it wasn't so fucking tragically ironic, I would laugh. The hinge pin of humanity turns out to be the very worst example of it.'

Barrett's head was spinning. The nausea had morphed into light-headedness, and despite being sat, cross legged on the floor, he felt like he was about to faint.

'I know the contents of your brief. Christ, I've known for over a year. I was tasked long before you were brought on-board. The meetings, the history lessons...shit, even the French tuition...' He paused to look down at Renton. 'But no amount of prep could have readied me for that...'. Barrett was struggling to breathe. He reached up to pull his collar wide. Sumner noticed, giving an empathetic smile.

'Truly, Liam, I wish I could have told you. Maybe if they'd planned things differently, we could have worked as a team.' He sighed.

The whirls of light around Barrett's head started to subside. He reached down with his hands, either side of him, feeling the rough grain of the wood with his fingertips. Needing to feel something stable. His mouth was like a desert, and he moved his tongue around in his mouth, trying to generate some saliva. At last, he feebly croaked out a single word.

'Why?'

Sumner hopped down from the bale and began to slowly walk around.

'Why, is a question I have been asking for the last few days, my friend. It's a question that I can't answer, for myself anyway. As for your question of 'why'...well...I was the 'back-up' plan. The 'just-in-case' alternative. A task that had such an importance, for our continued survival, could not be left to just one man alone.' Barrett could picture, almost hear, Anders uttering the words, walking around his board room table. 'As I said, *you* were the detective. The ideal person selected to 'sniff out' whether anyone had it in for our dear captain...' At this, Sumner erupted into a coughing laugh. 'I mean...who would wish harm on him? Such a gentle soul...' he reached for the canteen from Barrett, taking a quick swig to ease his retches.

Having calmed himself, he continued.

'You were there to identify the risks...the possible suspects that might want to kill him. I was there to make sure you could see things through; to step in, to assist, should the need arise. Sort of a guardian angel, behind the scenes, as it were. There was just one problem with the theory. They had underestimated...him.' He stopped to give Renton another kick.

'They had no idea what a monster he was; how could they know?' He squatted down, next to the captain, reaching out a hand to roughly grasp his hair, pulling his head up from the flooring. 'As you deduced...eventually...his discovery of my...orientation, put an end to any help I could possibly render.' He stared venomously at Renton's impassive face. 'We knew, of course, that being anything other than heterosexual during this time period was seen as a heinous crime, but it was never anticipated that it would ever present a problem...' His grin was humourless as he said: 'The planners didn't see that one coming did they? I don't imagine a visit to a whore house factored highly on their likely, computer-generated scenarios.' He let go of the head, which thumped unceremoniously upon the wood. 'As soon as he had me labelled as queer, he went out of his way to throw everything at me...' Sumner's voice had dropped in volume as he continued to stare at his nemesis' blanching, bloodless face. '...even forcing me to become a murderer.'

With surprising swiftness, Sumner stood and aimed the revolver at Renton's head. The cocking lever was moving backwards. The look in his eyes no longer betrayed any emotion. It was a cold stare. It meant nothing. Barrett shouted loudly.

'Lionel, NO!'

Sumner continued to point the weapon. But he did not fire.

'Why?' He glared at Barrett. 'Don't tell me any of that bullshit about the timeline. If this is what it means to exist as a species, we fucking don't deserve to.' He re-focused on Renton, the gun was aimed at his forehead.

Barrett started to uncross his legs, hoping they wouldn't let him down after feeling so weak, a moment ago.

'I don't care about that now, Lionel.' Pulling his right leg around, into a sprinter's crouch. 'We don't get to decide the future. It's never been about us, don't you see?' Sumner maintained his posture; he hadn't noticed Barrett's change in position. '...we were given a job...that's all it was...' He tensed his thighs, preparing for the lunge. But first he needed the gun to be pointed in another direction. Right now, one pull of the trigger, and Renton was gone.

'Is he a fucking monster? Yes...no...who fucking cares? Do you think he's the worst we can create? Trust me, Lionel, he doesn't even come close. Humanity is cruel, always has been. I don't know how he affects the future, and I don't think we'll ever know, but...'

Now...

'...you're willing to sacrifice every human life? Why? Because he pissed you off? Made you cry...like a fucking baby?'

It was supremely unjust. It had to be.

The revolver started to move, coming around in an arc, away from Renton…

...towards him.

Barrett launched himself with all his might. He didn't feel the cramp in his legs, didn't feel the dagger-like heat of the bullet rip past his shoulder, shaving the tiniest piece of skin off, as it passed by, didn't even feel his neck compressing as his head ploughed into Sumner's midriff. The two men crashed into a thick wooden beam, bracing the barn's wall. Their combined weight struck the wood with a bone crunching force, winding Barrett, causing him to lie for a moment, trying to recover. A moment, he knew, he didn't have to spare.

He needn't have worried. Sumner wasn't going anywhere. As Barrett pulled himself up to a kneeling position, he looked down at his fellow traveller. Sumner's mouth was opening and closing rapidly, like a fish landed out of water, his hands laying by his sides, convulsively twitching with firing motor neuron spasms. Barrett had seen this before. Sumner's neck was broken. The young man's eyes were piercing. Aflame. Barrett gripped one of his hands, crouching low to speak into his ear.

'I'm sorry, Lionel. You know I didn't mean any of that.' Sumner appeared to become calmer. His mouth slowly formed into a smile. Barrett went on. 'I need to get you to a medic. You've got to hang on, Lionel.' And then, as an afterthought: 'We need to get home.'

Sumner whispered something inaudible. Barrett brought his head closer, his ear pressing against Sumner's lips.

'Don't be naive.' He whispered again.

Then he was dead.

Northern France, September 10th, 1917

10:30 hrs.

Against all the odds, Renton lived.

Three French medical orderlies had wrapped the captain into a large thick sheet, forming a sausage shape which enabled his body to be safely and carefully passed down the through the dovecot hatch, and then stretchered out to the waiting horse-drawn ambulance. Some twenty minutes later, he was safely ensconced in the local hospital, two drips feeding his veins: one saline, the other, a life-saving infusion of his blood type, identifiable, fortunately, from his dog tags; the only thing on his person that had distinguished him as British Army.

Barrett sat on the pavement outside the ward, staring into the dust of the street. Simone was beside him, clinging to his arm, her head resting against his shoulder. He was exhausted. So fatigued, he could barely see straight. As worn out as he was, though, the smell of Simone's perfume permeated his nose, enlivening a part of him that had no right to make a claim on any of his remaining energy.

After Sumner has died, Barrett had sprinted back to Le Jardin, bursting in through the front doors, scaring the cleaning maids senseless. Simone had, at once, summoned the janitor to quickly bring the doctor, a wizened old man who, on surveying Renton's forlorn body, had at first simply shaken his head with resignation. It was understandable, the big man was a shadow of his former self. Barrett didn't think he had a single drop of blood left in him, his skin was so translucent. However, as the doctor performed a cursory check of the wound, the 'body' had coughed weakly.

Simone had led Barrett back to her room in the bordello. He'd followed her dutifully, as he had done on their first meeting. She'd fed him, bathed him, and turned down her bed for him to fall into. As he'd tried to pull her in with him, she had resisted, 'shushing' him kindly, and whispering:

'Rest.'

And rest he did.

Sleep had come to him, but it was hardly peaceful. Almost in a drug-like state, Barrett had spent hours tossing and turning, waking, in the middle of the night, coated in sweat; sometimes crying out; sometimes searching out in the dark with his hands, finding Simone, holding him close. She had calmed him. Laid him back down, so that he could drift off, once more, into the depths.

Late into the third day, in the bordello, he awoke to find Simone sitting on the bed, next to him, bathing his forehead with a warm, damp cloth. He sat up a little on his elbows, feeling a good deal brighter. This feeling was improved further, as she told him what he'd missed, in his convalescence.

'The town has been very full today. The rioters have all been...swept up? Now it is only marching soldiers. They tell us that the mutiny is over, it is...errr...squashed, no?' He chuckled, correcting her English.

'Quashed...but, good enough.' He tried to get up, but she easily pushed him back down. His protests met with playful insistence. He wasn't ready yet, she said. He agreed, but he had to know how Renton was. She told him that she would drop in, not to visit, merely to enquire as to his recovery.

After she had left him, he'd pondered her news with more deliberation. The date, he noted, was September 12th He'd been out of it for two whole days! More importantly, it also meant that the mutiny had concluded a full three days earlier than history had first recorded. This was as he'd predicted; the increased severity from this version of events had generated a much swifter response from Britain. The execution of high-ranking officers would have created mass panic in Whitehall, Barrett imagined. This train of thought led him to also contemplate his last few hours with Sumner.

Anders had oversimplified the whole, time loop premise, with his ridiculous umbrella theory. He'd said that most occurrences, that differed with the original path of history, had little to no effect. But that clearly hadn't been the case here, he reflected. The mutiny, this time around, had been a far deadlier affair, even if it hadn't gone on for as long. The reason? Sumner. He wasn't supposed to have been on that bridge. His inability to peacefully deal with the mutineers was key. And *he* wouldn't have been there, were it not for Renton's despicably evil, homophobic victimisation. So, despite Anders waxing lyrical that time travel 'didn't work that way', here it was again, the same old temporal paradox that featured in all the science fiction of old.

His mind dwelled on Sumner for some minutes, thinking how Renton was so very nearly killed by one of the very men sent to ensure his safety. As Barrett contemplated his last moments with the *lieutenant,* he couldn't get the man's parting words out of his mind. As he'd died, he'd told Barrett not to be naive. This had to have been in response to one of two things Barrett had said to him. The first was in answer to getting him to a medic; Sumner was no fool, he must have known his injury was terminal. The second, however, Barrett felt was more likely. The notion of getting him home.

Of either of them getting home.

'Don't be so naive.'

He had never really believed the technobabble anyway. All the crap the American scientist had spouted about dematerialising, after the job was done. Barrett presumed this had been some poorly conceived effort at allaying his fears, giving him some false hope for getting back. If they had read his file as extensively as they said they had, they should have known that none of that was necessary.

Not for him.

Some hours later, Simone came back into the room, having returned from the hospital. She reported that one of the nurses she'd known from school had looked in on the captain. Apparently, he had been mending remarkably well. So well, in fact, that he'd become a pain to some of the staff. He'd heard the army had retaken the camp and town, and, consequently, had begun making demands, ostensibly related to his transfer to one of the camp medical facilities. His perpetual bellyaching had been effective, however, and the doctors had been only too happy to see the back of him.

'He is due to be moved tomorrow.' Simone said, ending her account. She looked searchingly into his eyes, as he smiled. 'Why is this man so important to you?'

Barrett turned his smile towards her. He grasped her hand, squeezing gently.

'I'll tell you, some day.' He said cryptically. Though clearly not satisfied, she nudged him a little to make some space on the bed. Climbing up next to him, she nuzzled into the underside of his chin. He could feel her warmth, the softness of her skin, the soapy smell from her hair. Lying next to her, for the first time in many years, he felt truly contented. And listening to her breathing, feeling the smooth and steady rise and fall of her chest, he started to feel his eyes droop. He fought it for a few minutes, but then admitted defeat. He was drifting back to sleep. Feeling his eyes rolling up into the back of their sockets, he had just enough reserve left to ask:

'Will you be here, when I wake up?'

He just heard a single, whispered word.

'Oui.'

Then, nothing.